"Lester's novel about a tenacious, well-traveled heroine of a certain age is replete with the profound and comical observations of a vivacious spirit." —*O, The Oprah Magazine*

"I absolutely loved *Lillian on Life*. It was a delight. The style of it so fresh and clever and subversive, and there's something very brave about it, especially for a first novel."
—Kate Atkinson, *New York Times*–bestselling author of *Life After Life* and *A God in Ruins*

"Dazzling . . . In short vignettes, Lillian looks back, drawing an impressionistic portrait of a bold life full of adventure—erotic and otherwise—in prose spiked with unflinching observations, riotous riffs and poignant reflections." —*The Washington Post*

"Illuminating . . . The novel is a cleverly executed feminist bildungsroman that you could easily share with your mother, sister, friend, or, probably most appropriately, life coach." —*Nylon*

"What a great voice, what energy and wit. I enjoyed Lillian's travels, her various jobs, and her lovers. She had moments of great wisdom—I was drawn especially to those—and in the midst of the humor and the happenings, a sentence or two of such profundity. I thought the book was very original and often extremely funny, but always with an edge. My favorite kind of humor. I completely loved it!"
—Karen Joy Fowler, PEN/Faulkner Award winner and *New York Times*–bestselling author of *The Jane Austen Book Club*

"*Lillian on Life* is a quirky book with a very deep heart and soul. I found it full of life and full of wisdom."
—Erica Jong, *New York Times*–bestselling author of *Fear of Flying*

"A remarkably confident debut . . . Unconventionally plotted, Lillian's tale is filled with lush details and cool observations about the twins of female freedom: contentment and compromise. A slim novel that feels just perfect—each thought measured, each syllable counted, a kind of haiku to an independent woman."

—*Kirkus Reviews* (starred review)

"In this remarkably mature first novel, Alison Jean Lester has channeled the worldly yet wistful elegance of Colette to portray an unforgettable heroine. Lillian's provocative reflections on love, vanity, sexual intimacy, and surviving as an independent woman over half a century are deeply moving."

—Julia Glass, National Book Award–winning author of *Three Junes* and *And the Dark Sacred Night*

"Lillian is the cosmopolitan aunt we all wish we had—the one who always bestows the best advice just when it's needed, knows the perfect gift to give for every occasion, and tells the most interesting stories about her life. . . . Lester has given readers the grand gift of Lillian's wisdom, beauty, and candor in this lovely novel."

—*Booklist*

"What a splendid book! By turns acerbic and warm, urbane and homespun, *Lillian on Life* is—like its protagonist—charming, funny, and unabashedly smart. But as slender and enjoyable as this book is, it's much more than simply a lark. Each elegantly compressed chapter leaves us luxuriating in thought: about the snippets of experience so vividly depicted, and about those that have been, with perfect art, left out."

—Leah Hager Cohen, author of *The Grief of Others* and *No Book but the World*

"I'll never forget *Lillian on Life*. Looking backward, she's brutally honest about her needs, her lovers, her parents. Salinger could have invented her. . . . Roth would have loved her . . . and so will you. A rare book, a little raunchy, but very rich and very real."

—Ilene Beckerman, author of *Love, Loss, and What I Wore*

LILLIAN ON LIFE

G. P. PUTNAM'S SONS

New York

LILLIAN
ON LIFE

Alison Jean Lester

P U T N A M

G. P. PUTNAM'S SONS
Publishers Since 1838
An imprint of Penguin Random House LLC
375 Hudson Street
New York, New York 10014

The Library of Congress has catalogued the G. P. Putnam's Sons hardcover edition
as follows:

Lester, Alison Jean.
Lillian on life / Alison Jean Lester.
p.   cm.
ISBN 978-0-399-16889-5
1. Middle-aged women—Fiction.   2. Reminiscing—Fiction.
3. Autobiographical memory—Fiction.   4. Life change events—Fiction.
5. Man-woman relationships—Fiction.   6. Psychological fiction.   I. Title.
PS3612.E8193L55   2014   2013039008
813'.6—dc23

First G. P. Putnam's Sons hardcover edition / January 2015
First G. P. Putnam's Sons trade paperback edition / May 2016
G. P. Putnam's Sons trade paperback ISBN: 978-0-425-27620-4

Printed in the United States of America
1   3   5   7   9   10   8   6   4   2

Book design by Gretchen Achilles
Cover design by Gabriele Wilson
Cover illustration by Leanne Shapton

CONTENTS

On the Dual Purpose of Things

Whenever I wake up next to a man, before I'm fully awake, I think it's Ted. Of course it never is.

That's okay. This morning I watched Pandora walk the length of Michael's naked body. His skin turned to gooseflesh as she started up his thigh. Her pretty gray paw depressed the flesh of his belly, and his sleeping penis rolled toward his hipbone. She stepped off him at the shoulder. She could have walked on the bed; there was a little space between him and me. Maybe he doesn't exist for her. Maybe she was saying that he's no better than a mattress. She snuggled into my neck, purring smugly like an idling Jaguar.

I wanted Michael to wake up and see us like that: an independent woman beloved of her elegant cat. But of course he didn't. They don't. They wake up at all the wrong times, and see all the wrong things.

To be fair, we drank a lot of red wine last night, and I can hold it better than most people. My eyes still snap open in the morning. Wine is still my friend. I hate that I can't drink coffee in the wee hours and then sleep anymore, though. The body evolves, then it devolves. It's terrible. One day you're someone you know, and the next you're someone you don't. You dry up. It's embarrassing.

Every once in a while I wonder if I'm glad Ted didn't stick around for my menopause. A woman has so many things to hide after fifty. I ask myself if we could have tolerated so much physical change, followed by dotage.

I don't have to wonder with Michael. He comes and goes. There isn't time for him to notice everything.

The trick at my age is to keep some K-Y Jelly in an attractive pot on the bedside table. You squeeze it out of the tube into the pot for when you have a visitor. When his hands are beginning to move on you, you turn away and slip your fingers into the jelly. He can caress your bottom or your shoulders in the meantime. When you turn back you take him in your hand and lubricate him. Maybe he's not even erect yet, and this way you have the satisfaction of knowing that what you're doing for him is working. I'm not sure there's a bigger satisfaction than that in life. And as long as he's feeling it's for him, you've diverted his attention—and even your own—from the fact that the lubrication is for you. On top of it all you maintain your sense that you've still got plenty of sap in your tree. Name me a wife who does that.

Michael's wife is crazy. She probably didn't seem it when

she was young. She probably just seemed young. Now she just seems silly. That hair band of hers. The tangential things she says. She's almost as tall as I am, and only about five years younger, fifty-two I think, but she blinks at you. She stands up tall and her chestnut hair sits perfectly turned up on her shoulders in the same way I'm sure it has since 1960, and she smiles and blinks, as if to protect herself from anything modern or unpleasant. Imagine life by her side. How would you ever connect? Well, you wouldn't.

Do some people not need excitement? I've always thought humans were too complicated not to need stimulation. What does Michael do to keep his wife hanging on? Or what does she do that keeps him married to her? I don't like to ask. I've learned not to cling.

He sleeps really late when he's with me. I don't think it's allowed at home, certainly not naked. He's intimated as much. Separate beds too.

I thought my parents' marriage had come to an end the day their twin beds arrived. I didn't know it was happening all over the neighborhood, probably all over the country, and Mother was merely keeping up with the Joneses. But how often did the Joneses go up to my parents' bedroom? Never. Mother just felt them walking around in her head, and had to keep up.

I got up when my stomach started rumbling. Thank God Michael sleeps through that too. Accommodating Pandora was giving my neck a cramp. I wanted my usual breakfast: milk so skim it's almost blue, a banana, an English muffin with a thin slice of cheese, black coffee. The breakfast I like happens to be excellent for the bones and muscles and digestion of a woman my age. I think just about everything has a dual purpose, like K-Y Jelly.

It's lonely eating alone when there's someone in the house, but then again, you can use the bathroom and get that all out of the way before they get up. The advantage to not living with a man is that you avoid each other's smells. For the most part, Michael moves his bowels elsewhere. I learned early on to keep matches in my cosmetics kit for when I was "visiting," and in my toilet when being visited. You light one and guide the flame around the inside of the toilet right after flushing. You won't burn yourself if you hold the match between the first joints of your index and middle fingers like a tiny cigarette. Then you wash your hands thoroughly. Since the sink is usually closer to the door than the toilet, anyone entering the bathroom after you will smell soap before they smell anything else.

Mary taught me this back in Missouri. Poppa's bathroom had bright sun in it in the morning, a small TV, eventually, and a box of matches on the windowsill that she had put there. This was one of the many reasons I could list as a child why black people were superior. They were clearly the smart ones; we obviously couldn't cook without them, and that was just the beginning.

I loved hearing Mary in the bathrooms when I woke up in the mornings. In Poppa's, she opened the window and flapped and refolded the towels, then there'd be a quiet moment and that was when she was using a match in the toilet bowl. Poppa's "time" was right after his early breakfast and his second cup of coffee. After airing his toilet, Mary'd sing down the hall to my room, where I'd pretend to sleep, and sometimes she'd sit down heavily on the end of the bed and feign surprise that I was there. "Still in bed, missy!" she'd say. "You get on out of there or you'll end up being too beautiful, it's the truth." Then she'd get up and cross the room to my bathroom. "I'd best clean your mirror so you can have a look-see at your too-beautiful self," she'd say, or something like it.

I wonder if beauty has a dual purpose.

No. It has no purpose, and offers no guarantees. In my experience, beauty merely has a dual result: one, lots of people talk to you; two, nice photographs.

A wife's got to serve a dual purpose. Michael's doesn't.

On the
Back Seat

The first car I remember was a Studebaker Champion. Corky's family eventually got one too, and theirs was a pale sea green, aquamarine in the bright sunshine, and I envied the color. Ours was tan, however the sun was shining, but it was the first in our neighborhood of Columbia, Missouri. I felt sorry for Mother that she always sat in the front and never got to sit behind Poppa and watch him drive. You can't see that much of people nowadays because the seat backs and headrests come up so high. Also because steering wheels are smaller now. When Poppa bought that car it must have been 1948 or so—yes, it was; I remember because I was fifteen and Mother had allowed me to get my ears pierced when I turned fifteen, and I always made sure I had earrings on to go out in the car. The steering wheel was a smooth wide circle, set up high, and when Poppa drove I could see his head and neck and shoulders and hands, and the Freemason's ring that flashed on his right pinkie.

George Junior got that ring when Poppa died. I have the diary he kept during the war, somewhere, and his Purple

Heart medal too. He wrote about advancing across French fields with his friends falling and dying to his right and left. I knew about that already because Mother told me. He kept writing in his diary after the war as well, when he was back in Hannibal with his parents and his sisters and wondering where to go from there. He met Mother in church. He didn't mention that in his diary, though. He wrote about her only when he already knew her a little. "I don't know what it is," he put down in his slightly cramped hand. "When I'm with Vivian I have a feeling in my chest that I can't name. It's a tightness, and I have a notion that she can relieve it."

Did she? He looked contented enough, despite the limitations of twin beds and the lipstick she always put on before coming downstairs in the morning, marking the end of kisses for the day. She could receive them, of course, and would always proffer a cheek when any of us came home. She'd pat me on the bottom instead. I don't remember her kissing Poppa, though.

"I have a feeling in my chest." It was so strange reading those words, knowing that when he wrote them he hadn't declared himself to her yet, knowing that by the time I read them hundreds and thousands of moments had passed between my parents that I had never perceived and would never understand, or even accept. Their relationship seemed to function along the lines of a pattern. To learn that, at least for him, it started with the shortness of breath and a desire for sweet relief, well, I had to think about that. And when I thought about that, standing there three years ago in my dining room next to the box of Poppa's things I'd opened on the table, I got angry. She just hadn't appreciated him. When I think of my young self sitting on the back seat of the Studebaker, watching him drive so elegantly around town while she looked out the window and commented on the houses, I know I was in the right place. I used to put my hand on his shoulder to remind him I was there.

On How
to Study

Where'd I put the crossword puzzle? I thought I'd finish it while I ate, but I couldn't find it, not the one I was working on anyway. Where is it? God. It's always like this. Stupid, Lillian. Stupid. Think. Focus.

In high school I was never one to do my homework with the other girls. I have no idea how they got it done that way. You have to be quiet, sharpen your pencils, get the right paper, put your head down. I did homework in my room in the late afternoon, after a Coke with Mary in the kitchen. Poppa would come home around five thirty, unless he was traveling, and there was usually a good forty-five minutes when I'd be composing something at my desk and Poppa would be in his office next to my parents' bedroom calculating something, looking at what he'd written on the little pieces of paper he always had folded in half in the pocket of his shirt. I felt a real freshness in my brain then. A clarity of focus. A breeze. Whatever I wrote was speedy and solid. Whatever I read made sense. I came up with ideas for term papers. I drew accurate graphs. Then Poppa would clear his throat. Funny how men do this when they stop concentrating, at the end of a project. This was the sign. It was time for him to make drinks. Mother was waiting downstairs with her hand already curved to receive her bourbon. That's how she looked, sitting in the sunroom at the end of the day, lipstick renewed, waiting for things to happen the way they were supposed to happen.

At dinner, I know Poppa liked me to talk about my schoolwork, but he'd always offer Mother an opportunity to talk first. "Shall we find out what Vivi Anne has to say about the world today?" he'd ask me, and I'd consider the question, and nod. Her name was Vivian. I never asked him why he played with the pronunciation. I assumed it was because she wasn't the kind of woman you tickled with your fingers. It was a funny way to tease and show respect at the same time, calling her Vivi Anne, letting her have the floor first, listening as if he truly cared or would remember which store was having a sale.

I couldn't really think without Poppa nearby. It was as if my brain were a boat, and when I left home for Vassar I left my anchor behind rather than pulling it up and dropping it in the new place. My brain kept sneaking out of the harbor. It all had to do with hands. Phone calls and hands.

The calls started on Wednesday evenings. Just a couple

would come in, usually for the same girls, but sometimes there was a surprise, and then on Thursday evening there were lots more, and any girl without a date for the weekend would go to class on Friday morning with a heavy heart even though there was still time.

The phone was quiet for the first few weeks of my first year, so I spent most evenings in the library rather than listening for the phone at the entrance to the residence hall. I was there to study, after all. I'd signed up for more than the required number of credits, in order to do a double major—early childhood education and English literature. Lots of girls were doing a major and a minor, or even a major and two minors. But what kind of word is that, *minor*? A minor in religion, or philosophy? It's like taking only a thin slice of fruitcake. What if the cherry is on the other side of the cake and you never taste it? I was too hungry for that.

On the wall by my bed I'd stuck up a schedule I'd made for myself showing how many hours a day I needed to devote to each class, and it looked perfectly doable, and I threw myself into it with my sharpened pencils and my notebooks and my belief that pretty little Vassar meant me no harm. But then, after some of the girls took me along to a dinner and dance at Yale, the calls started coming in for me as well. I'd try to study in the bedroom, but in fact I'd just be waiting like we all were, and my roommate, Ann, would start playing with her hair. She was a serious student. I couldn't understand a word of the economics books she loved so much. Well, no, I could, but my eyes crossed, literally crossed, when I took a look at them. That made her laugh. Ann. Nice girl. She was one of the earliest women on Wall Street. She's still there, I believe. J.P.Morgan, I think. She had long straight hair, and was fond of saying she couldn't do a thing with it, and on Wednesday and Thursday nights while we waited to hear the phone ring, she'd start by taking it out of its ponytail while we were studying, and then inevitably she'd twirl it around her finger, and that would distract us both, and one of us would pull out a magazine to look at styles, or she'd stand in front of the mirror and I'd watch her, and we'd both imagine her on a date.

The phone calls threw off my study schedule completely. I told myself to get up early on Sundays and go back to the library. Sometimes I was able to, sometimes not. I told myself to keep to the evening study schedule, to let someone else take any call that came in for me and take a message, and sometimes I was able to, but I'd come home early. Sunday nights I fell asleep in the stacks.

Hands. Yale men knew where to put them. First date: elbow, early in the evening, on the way into a restaurant; between the shoulders, lightly, on the way out. Second date: small of the back. Just a tad possessive, just a tad suggestive, with an I-know-which-way-to-take-us quality that was always encouraging, even when you had an inkling it was insincere. Third date: waist, or hand. Neck. Neck when they kissed you, fingers meeting on your nape, under your hair, thumbs in front of your ears. Eventually: hip, thigh. That was nice. It wasn't supposed to happen too early, and it was supposed to happen in conversation, maybe when they leaned toward you to deliver a punch line or point, so that it wasn't too raw, too frank. The ones who barely touched me at all on the first date—holding a door with no need to put a hand on me to usher me through it—reminded me of Poppa, and I liked them for it, but not if it lasted too long.

Come to think of it, when Poppa held a door for Mother and me, we'd both let Mother go through first, then I'd go through, and he'd touch me. He always touched me when I went through a door.

There were other hands distracting me, early in my second year, when those of us studying early childhood education were placed in nursery schools for experiential training. When I got back to our room at the end of those days, I was the one standing in front of the mirror, playing with my hair, picking the glue out of it, showing off the finger paint under my nails, telling stories of adoration and frustration, but most of all remembering the little hands on me. It felt like all the energy of the world was coming to me through the tiny palms the children would place on my calves to steady themselves or get my attention. I was supposed to put them down at naptime and teach them to calm themselves, but I couldn't. I'd keep one or another in my arms on some pretense—I couldn't get a shoe untied, I needed to wipe a runny nose—just to feel them go a little heavier in my arms and see that final instinctive reach toward my neck as I put them down and they allowed sleep to take over. Their hands gave me goose bumps.

There was one little girl named Joan. She was the tiniest one in the group, with soft dark ringlets that reminded me of me, and a methodical approach to playing that kept her one step behind the other babies. I was standing in the doorway one breezy October day, watching the others play on the little playground and also waiting for Joan to finish lining up all the dollies so they could go to sleep. A few times before, she had just pushed unsteadily past me through the door when she was done, but this time she patted the back of my knee, and when I turned around she had her arms up and her head tipped all the way back, throat exposed and pulsing, the way little children do to signal that they really mean it and they'll probably make a fuss if you don't agree. It was as if we'd already been communicating, and she was just taking it up a notch. "Oh, sugar," I said as I picked her up and sat her on my hip. "You all worn out from putting your babies to bed?" She just looked out at the playground, and seemed contented to stay and look, her body still, not leaning forward and kicking the way some of the children did to make you go somewhere. So I looked too. We stood in the doorway like mother and child, like wife and child looking out from a home, keeping a watchful eye on the rest of the family playing. Her left arm was behind my shoulder, and after a while I felt her little fingers idly exploring the hair at the back of my neck.

Goose bumps.

We all had a meeting with the head of the department at the end of that term to discuss the feedback from the teachers we had been assisting, and to receive our next assignment. Her name was Mrs. Wade. She wore wire-rimmed glasses and no makeup at all. She resembled an aging movie actor, Spencer Tracy maybe, in sort of the way Margaret Mead's face was a practice run for Anthony Hopkins. She had square gray teeth, and bright eyes. She told me she'd received a glowing report and that I was clearly well suited to the purpose of helping children learn and grow. There was a little bit of concern regarding my use of time.

"You mean I wasn't efficient?"

"More that you didn't check the clock quite often enough," she said. "Do you recall having to be reminded that it was time for another activity, or lunch, quite a lot?"

I thought. "Maybe. A few times. But Mrs. Wade," I said, "the babies! I couldn't take my eyes off them to look up at the clock; they were just too sweet and interesting. I didn't want to miss a single thing. If they could ring bells or something when we are supposed to change our activities, then maybe I could be more attentive."

Mrs. Wade laughed. "An excellent idea, Lillian. It's interesting that you refer to them as babies, dear. The youngest would have been two, I'm sure."

"Babes in the woods, then," I said. "Innocents."

I saw Mrs. Wade's eyebrows twitch down at this, but she smiled again. "Fair enough. Anyway! Well done. And on to a kindergarten class now, where the youngest will be five, and most of the children will be six."

Suddenly my tongue tingled with a panic I usually reserved for standing up to speak in class. "Can't I stay at the nursery school?" I blurted.

"No, dear. You've got to do next term in a kindergarten, just like all the others."

"How about a couple of hours a week?"

Mrs. Wade folded her hands on the desk in front of her. "What for?" she asked.

"For the babies," I said. "We know each other now. Won't it, I mean, isn't it hard for them to adjust to new people all the time?"

"Hard for the children?"

"Yes!"

"It would be difficult if their teacher changed every term, yes, but as it's only the assistant that changes, and they know it's going to happen, it seems to be fine. Anyway, Lillian," she said, unclasping her hands and pulling my file into her lap, "I can't see a gap in your schedule here that would allow for extra time in a nursery school."

I don't remember what was said after that. I returned to my room with a piece of paper in my hand, giving me the details of my kindergarten assignment, but I couldn't look at it. I stood and stared out the window. Did six-year-olds hang on to your neck? I didn't think so. I couldn't bear it.

That evening in the library I tried to continue with my reading of *Methods for the Study of Personality in Young Children*, but all the flavor had gone out of the meal. The next morning, I didn't get up. I think I went to class once or twice in the next two weeks, but I wasn't really there. One afternoon Ann came and found me sitting under one of the big trees by the chapel. When she pulled me to my feet and put her arm around my shoulders I realized I was cold. I don't know how long I'd been sitting there. It was hard to think.

I went home to Columbia and started at the University of Missouri. Just English lit this time.

I'll have children of my own, I told myself. *I don't need to take care of other people's.*

My class schedule didn't allow me to be home at the same time every day. I had to study after dinner, which worked very well when Mother was watching television in the sunroom and Poppa was reading the evening paper in his chair in the living room. There were times when I would sit down with my books and sigh and run my hands through my hair before starting, and Poppa would get up, come over to where I was sitting, slide off my shoes and massage my feet. He didn't slide both my shoes off at once. He'd take one off and massage that foot, and the other foot would stay on the floor like a girl on the edge of a dance, waiting to be noticed and chosen. With both thumbs he'd press the ball of my foot, spreading my toes out slowly. He squeezed both sides of the foot from the top, from the ankle and toward him to the toe. He'd always finish by placing the mount of Venus of one hand against the arch of my foot, and curving his other hand over the top of the foot, closing me in, warming my blood, always taking care with every movement.

Did Mother let him do that for her? I think there was quite a lot Mother didn't let Poppa do. Poor Poppa. His hands were so strong and sensitive. He didn't talk when he massaged my feet. He just looked at them.

The way I saw it, the reason we didn't really suffer during the Depression was that my father was so handsome. As a silver salesman in Missouri and beyond, he shouldn't have been able to make a good living. Doors shouldn't have opened to him, but they did. I'm almost sure Poppa was faithful, but the image of him in the sitting rooms of pretty Missouri housewives, giving and receiving the flattery and pleasure that weren't common currency at home, was too sweet to discard. After all, it was thanks to them that Mother had the house, the Wedgwood, the bourbon, the cigarettes, the weekly dress money, the silent grand piano. George Junior's piano. I had piano lessons too, of course. Dance lessons first, though, to go with the ringlets. Mother insisted I was going to be the next little Shirley Temple.

Later there was piano, and singing. I had perfect pitch. I've lost it by a half step lately, but it's a perfect half step. So I could play piano, and did, but only when I was sure Mother was upstairs or out and wouldn't come and stand in the bay of the baby grand and get all mushy about how George Junior used to play whenever she asked him to, even for guests, before he left for California.

She was right. He was wonderful at the piano. He still is. It's just that perfect pitch didn't mean a thing to Mother. There's nothing as perfect as a talented firstborn son who has gone away.

When he went to North Carolina for training, near the end of the war, it felt so far away that he might as well have gone to France. I was twelve. I started knitting argyle socks right away, like we all did. Well, sock. I could never just pick it up and get back to work on it in the evenings. The instructions defied me. If I looked away from my knitting to consult them, I was completely lost when I looked back at it. Eventually I finished the sock, but the war was ending, so I wrapped it up and sent it off to him, just in case he needed one replacement sock or something. The letter that came back was mocking. There was no chimney to hang it on, he said, and it wasn't even Christmas anyway. A woman would have felt something positive, receiving one hand-made sock. A sister would. I never sent gifts in half measures after that, ever.

Professors didn't like half measures either, I learned. They saw inconsistent work as inconsistent effort, which was never the case. There were just days when I'd sit in the library with the perfect pencil and a notebook with lines ruled just the way I like, and they might as well have been a twig and a stone. Nothing would happen. I'd turn in a stilted, hard-won paragraph or two. Professorial eyes would roll. Professorial lower lips would jut. "Lillian," they'd say, "what happened? You can do so much better." They ganged up, too. I was walking through Main Building to get back to my room sometime in the middle of that first winter, bundled up and sniffing to keep my nose from dripping, when I turned a corner into a trio of women: Mrs. Wade; a beige woman I didn't know holding an armful of files; and Miss Blanding, the college president. "Is that you, Lillian?" Mrs. Wade said. "How funny, because we were just talking about you."

"Speak of the devil," I said, sniffing.

"Not at all," said Miss Blanding, taking control in her tailored black wool and bold silver choker. Her Kentucky accent caught me off guard. I'd heard her voice before, but not at such close quarters. I'd been working to minimize my Missouri accent and did pretty well at it until someone from the Midwest or the South stepped into the conversation. "Not the devil at all," she continued. "Just an intelligent girl trying to make her way in the world, isn't that right?"

"I don't know about intelligent," I said, fighting the urge to tack "Ma'am" onto the end. "Trying to make her way toward a heat source, anyway."

The three of them laughed, and I started to relax, and then Mrs. Wade cleared her throat and said, "We were talking about girls who have a . . . shall we say complicated? . . . relationship with concentration."

"Oh," I said. Mrs. Wade carried on when I couldn't think of anything else to say.

"We're wondering how to help." She and the other woman raised their eyebrows to show they were open to suggestions, but Miss Blanding seemed to be assessing me. When I didn't talk, Miss Blanding said, "Do you exercise?"

"I do phys ed, like all the girls," I answered.

"Exercise does wonders for the mind, you know."

I nodded.

She stepped back to take me in from boots to hat. "Basketball might be your sport," she concluded.

"Maybe it is," I said, twinkling at the eyes, as if I thought Miss Blanding's idea was brilliant. I made to move around them. "It would probably keep me warm," I said.

"That's the spirit," said Miss Blanding, sounding as if she felt the meeting had been very successfully concluded, but Mrs. Wade called after me. "Come and see us anytime, Lillian. We're here to help."

I couldn't bear the idea that I was being talked about. Worried about. Couldn't bear it. I bought a marker pen and highlighted the hours in my study schedule that I was determined to make sacrosanct. But when I tried to study, my brain literally felt like a damp bathing suit, and I was wringing it and wringing it, but the water was distributed too finely through the fibers to come together into droplets. I couldn't drench the page with thoughts, only smudge it. I did fine in high school. I did well. College rocked my confidence. Except with men. I'm so glad I went north to college, for that reason alone, even though I had to leave early. At the evening socials organized with Yale, I met young men older than I was, and taller, but more importantly, young men with a more sophisticated charm, men who didn't squirm in a tweed blazer and who told me I looked beautiful rather than swell.

Professors were frightening. Men weren't.

On Getting
to Sex

Corky has only had sex with one man in her entire life. But she got to sex so much earlier than I did. One moment we were girls in bobby socks finishing up the school year, the next moment we were at camp in Wisconsin and I was walking down the path to the lake and she was crashing toward me through the bushes. She had her sandals in her hands. Her feet must have been sore from running out of the woods, but she didn't stop to put her sandals on. When she reached me she was grinning, her chest was heaving, her eyes and cheeks were glowing. I fixated on her soft brown curls as she talked. Her hair was extremely soft, like a little child's, but the rest of her was a locomotive, whistle hooting, steam hissing.

"You have *got* to let a fella touch you like that," she panted as we headed to the lake.

"Like what?"

Corky just kept panting.

"What did he touch?"

"Everything," she crowed.

We walked a little. She knew I'd ask.

"With what?"

"With everything!"

She said it was "glorious." The path disappeared into the narrow beach. I took off my shoes and drew circles with my toes in the silt at the edge of the water. Corky tucked her skirt into her panties and walked in up to her knees, splashing water onto her face and thighs with both hands. You'd think she'd grown up on a farm, but her father was dean of physical sciences at the University of Missouri.

Corky was my best friend, but sometimes I felt this was by default. I really wished I were good friends with Mary Cate Myers. She was such an elegant girl, and so nice to everyone. She always did the right thing. I'd watch as she chose a subject for a history paper or answered a question about cosines, and above all when other students talked to her. She was always pleased, or kindly amused, or genuinely concerned. She *knew*. She arranged her face right. Corky got to sex at the right time for Corky, but too early for me. I wasn't ready to hear about it. Mary Cate would have gotten to it at the right time for everybody, so no one would have been shocked.

Mother had been able to see I was anxious as the departure for camp approached. Maybe because I was being such a dodo about it. Mother had never been away to camp, but I kept asking her what it was like. Finally she asked me if there was someone in my class I especially admired for the way she behaved. Of course I said Mary Cate Myers. "Well," she said, "when you're unsure of what to do, just behave the way you think that girl would." So far it had worked a couple of times. I gave new people I met a warm Mary Cate smile, and if it was an adult I shook hands. I didn't wait for them to probe me; I asked them where they were from first. But with close friends it's tough. They're so far under your skin you can't push them back up to the surface and act like an acquaintance. They look at you funny. So I made circles in the silt.

It's so odd to look back on. Sex is so important. In high school and college, it was really important to me not to have it. Now it's just the opposite.

About five years ago George Junior called me at eleven at night to tell me his daughter, Zoë, had just told him she was going to spend the night at her new boyfriend's apartment. She must have been about twenty at the time. He didn't know what to do.

"But it's wonderful!" I told him.

George Junior's wife, Judy, was out of town. Zoë's birthday was coming up, so the next weekend I went out and bought her a pale salmon silk nightgown and a cotton kimono covered in large pastel flowers. When I gave them to her I told her they were for when she went "visiting" and twinkled my eyes at her. There's a scene in *Rear Window* where Grace Kelly shows up at Jimmy Stewart's ridiculous little apartment with a tiny case, and when she pops the clasp she releases a small cloud of whitest silk and a pair of feathered mules. I could imagine Zoë doing this, changing into something coolly attractive.

Doing it myself took me so long to achieve. People were always interrupting me, taking me by surprise. Women's underwear in the fifties was like armor. I'm sure that men's fantasy of removing it was much sexier than the reality. When a woman went into her room to change into bed wear, she left the man to imagine her slipping out of her dress, stockings, panties and bra, and he could see it however he wanted to. He didn't have to witness the permanent grime on the elastic or struggle with the hooks, which in those days almost always came in a line of three and were designed to stay resolutely put. While he sipped his drink, he could imagine something pale and cupped falling to the ground or being draped on the bed, then she would come out in her beautiful ensemble and he'd look up, and smile, and put down his drink, and come to her.

Except that so often he didn't. I'd open the door and he'd

be standing right by it and there would be no conversation, no toasts, no ceremony, just whiskey lips and five-o'clock shadow and the cold door frame against my spine. He'd be right there clasping me against him and I could watch the ice cubes melting in my drink, right next to his empty glass. Eventually I learned to take the drink into the bedroom or bathroom with me as I changed. If he even let me change. Some men didn't.

I'll admit something, though. When it did happen that I'd come back out in a negligee and peignoir, hair brushed and perfume renewed, and the man would hand me my drink and tell me what he'd been thinking while I was gone, something usually to do with company politics, I'd feel hurt. He acted as if my going away to slip into something more comfortable was simply a matter of my own preference. You'd think I'd come back into the room in a housedress and friendly old slippers. I never, ever understood how professional concerns could trump a blooming female body in silk. Never understood it. Everyone and everything about our society said the reality was otherwise. I thought career obligations were something men met when there was no flesh available for pressing. Once I had come around to sex and even presented myself on its platter, it was a shock to be turned away. Okay, not turned away. That didn't happen. But postponed. Once I'd heard the whole political story and the decks were cleared, then the man would notice what he had within reach on the couch. I often had the impression that I could see a man's eyes change color when they started to focus on the present, and the fact that I was throbbing in the center of it.

Ted taught me the sweet tension of having a constant sexual connection, work or no work. Even if he was thinking about work when we were alone, or needed to talk about work, he was touching me somehow. It helped him. It helped me. But that was a few decades after Corky came crashing toward me through the Wisconsin woods. Such a funny thing. She married that boy. They got older and he studied architecture and grew a mustache and needed thick glasses. Turned out he was a very fine sculptor, in bronze. Small, heavy bulls. Roaring lionesses. It's no surprise Corky treats each day as another opportunity to run around in shoeless wonderment.

On "Us"

Maybe I would have had sex with Dave after college back in Columbia, but the first time he hugged me, he squeezed me so hard I passed wind. I've had a lifelong dread of being the first one to fart in a relationship. The fact that Dave went on to propose marriage less than a month later should have put paid to that, but it didn't. George Junior doesn't realize how lucky he is sometimes. Judy thinks gas is hilarious. It annoys him, but he should be glad.

Dave said, "Oh no! I popped you!" and took responsibility for the embarrassing sound I made. Dave was impeccable. He was like the men in early Richard Avedon fashion shoots—as elegant and happy and delicious stepping out of a go-go bar as out of an embassy function.

"No, you didn't," I said, my face burning, and took his arm and pulled him along the dark sidewalk toward his car, in case there was a smell. "One day I will," he said quietly, and I laughed because of course I pretended to think he was still talking about me as a windbag when I could tell from his voice that he was speaking sexually.

When he kissed me at the door to my parents' house he breathed in through his nose like you would over a warm pie fresh from the oven, and then he sighed. "I want to meet your parents," he said.

"Now?" I asked.

"No," he said evenly.

"When?"

"When you also want me to," was his answer. I loved this about Dave. He was so fun and easygoing, and then suddenly he'd fix you with an honest stare and say things as straight as they could be said.

My parents wanted me to meet men who wanted to meet them. This was the whole point of all my activities, as far as I could tell. It had been very slim pickings until now, though, and it had taken a Vassar connection to bring David Carter Allen into my life. He was the older brother of a friend of a girl from college, and was at law school in New Haven. He'd come to St. Louis for the summer to intern at Hawk & Mattingly, and had been told to look me up.

It was a two-hour drive to Columbia on a good day, but having met me once he made the trip often. He even had to borrow a car each time. There were pretty girls in St. Louis. Career girls too. Every time I knew he was already on the road to come and see me, I had to talk to myself all over again about how it could be that he kept making the trip. The answer was problematic. During our first lunch and walk around the university quadrangle I asked him why he'd taken an internship in Missouri rather than New York or Washington. "I've been imagining a simpler life for myself, so I thought I'd come and see what that might be," he said. I remember nodding, looking at the ground, because St. Louis didn't seem simple at all to me. Crossing all that traffic always got me hot and bothered. But what did I know? And then he started visiting, making the drive on a Sunday, or even a Friday afternoon, and I started thinking that I might be right: Maybe St. Louis wasn't really that simple. Maybe Dave had decided he had to come all the way to Columbia for life to be as quiet as he thought he liked. Every time he was on his way to visit I thought about how he might want me to be cute and compliant, and I thought about how I would rather be interesting and tantalizing, and I didn't know what to do. I knew he was charming, though, and I knew he was handsome, and healthy, so I waited for him to arrive and hoped I could be cute when I was listening to him and interesting when I was doing the talking.

Mother took against him immediately when he came to dinner a few weekends after the fart. It seemed to be because he wasn't one of "us." But if she was so devoted to "us," why was she always insisting on cosmetic improvements? We were constantly upgrading. I imagined that she would be happy to think a well-bred young man like Dave would want an alliance, but after he had had dinner with us and left for the long drive back to the city, Mother started slamming things around in the kitchen. I picked up the cocktail glasses from the living room but hesitated to join her. Poppa was tidying the bar.

"I don't understand," I whispered to him.

He leaned sideways to whisper back, "I think next time he might consider calling her Ma'am."

Young men in Missouri were brought up to address their elders as "Ma'am" and "Sir" until invited to do otherwise. They'd expected the same from Dave, who had called them Vivian and George, as he'd been brought up to do in Connecticut. If we got married, he would be invited to call my parents Mother and Dad. Their first names were out of bounds for life, in fact. Dave hadn't thought to ask permission. I hadn't thought to explain to him. It was all new to us. We were so young.

Mother seemed more relaxed the next morning when I came down for breakfast. I stared blindly into the fridge, hoping she'd talk first.

"Well," she said, putting her cup on the table and sliding onto the bench of the nook, "Dave seems like he's going places."

"I'm sure he is," I said, and smiled, ignoring her tone. "He's also very fun, and kind. And he seems to really like Columbia."

"Uh-huh," she said, and I pulled out an orange. I stuck my thumbnail into it to start peeling, spraying myself in the eye with stinging skin juice. She said, "It would be kind of him to marry you."

"I'm sorry?" I said, blinking from the acid in the juice, and in her voice.

She made me wait while she sipped her Sanka. "No, actually, it would be *unkind* of him to marry you."

Where was Poppa?

"What are you trying to say to me, Mother?" I asked, feeling a prickly blossom of tears in my throat. I still had my thumb in the orange.

"I'm trying to say, Lillian, that you will feel like a fish out of water among his people."

"Oh, I'm sure they are just as warm as he is," I said.

She shrugged. "Suit yourself," she said, getting ready to take another sip. "Just don't come crying to me if he's cooled off a bit today after meeting us last night."

When we're young, we're unfit to judge whether our parents know what they're talking about. Sometimes we want them to be right, sometimes we want them to be dead wrong, but we can't tell which they are actually being. If we could figure out which instinct guided them, the terrain would be much easier to navigate. I couldn't tell if Mother was speaking from the instinct to protect me, or the instinct to protect herself. It was gruesome.

In any case, Dave hadn't cooled off at all. We went out to visit the Budweiser Clydesdales. Driving over, we had the windows down because the day was so warm and muggy. Dave had to shout to ask me how I thought dinner with my parents had gone. He was smiling and his normally neat and gleaming hair was flapping crazily every which way. I couldn't bring Mother's cutting comments into that sweet car. I squeezed his hand and smiled back. I didn't mind lying, but I didn't want to have to do it at high volume. He took my smile as an answer and went back to concentrating on the road.

We joined a tour. Walking from the ticket office toward the beautiful old stables with my hand in Dave's, lagging a bit behind the group, I experienced a wonderful shiver of anticipation, like the ones you get on the nights before Christmas when you step out of your house or out of a warm car and the full, sparkling force of the season hits you. I could marry a handsome northern lawyer, I was thinking. An enthusiastic and handsome northern lawyer. The shiver went up my trunk and into the roots of my hair. I squeezed Dave's hand again, really hard, to stop my scalp from popping off the top of my head. He squeezed back, and leaned over to steal a kiss, and we walked from the sun into the thick darkness of the stable.

We reassembled as a group to listen to the guide. As my eyes adjusted to the low light and my nose started to relax after the initial shock of straw, piss, leather and ripe maleness, the guide opened the half door of a stable to our right, motioned us to move back a bit and led a horse out. Dave pulled me around the side of the group to get closer. Clydesdales were originally bred in Scotland. That's all I can remember from the guide's spiel. That's all I remembered even on the day we went, because once the horse stood before us I felt like a child. We only came to his shoulder. The guide, who was quite short, invited volunteers to come forward and stand by the animal to let us all feel the shift in perspective. Dave stepped forward first, looking so pleased, and my sense of childishness intensified. All I wanted was to get back out into the sun and feel tall again. The guide made it possible for us all to touch the patient Clydesdale if we wished, one by one, and of course I got in line. I'm happy around horses, but when I stood at his head and reached up to place the palm of my hand on his muzzle, the softness between his enormous nostrils suddenly felt deceptive, like it might be quicksand.

We went to see the hitch, and Dave asked questions about how much the reins weighed when held together at one time, and it was a lot. "Wow," he said, "you'd have to really prepare yourself for that."

"Imagine lifting weights just to be able to control a team of horses," I said.

"Preparation is everything," he said.

We drove back to Columbia and went to lunch at the soda fountain near my house. On the way there I looked at Dave a lot. I studied his hands. They were grown-up hands. Were they elite hands? I thought so. Were they *elitist* hands? It had never crossed my mind. Sitting at the counter with our liverwurst sandwiches and root beer floats, like I had so often in high school, I didn't feel any better. Dave looked happy as a clam, but I felt hokey. The reason the men in Richard Avedon's fashion photos look so gorgeous in the seedy parts of Paris is that they're not from there. They're visiting, or they're leaving, having visited.

That was the summer the chance to work in Munich

came up. I didn't know anything about moving yet. I now know, from moving and moving and moving, that the only way to handle being asked to leave a country you love for another you don't know is to start looking forward immediately. If there's anything you've been meaning to buy, buy it, then pack it, and start imagining it on a new mantel or in a new closet. Start imagining yourself around new landmarks, investigating new supermarkets, tuning your ear to the new language.

I remember waking up on a Saturday morning that summer, not long after Dave's proposal, to the sounds of neighborhood lawn mowers. Suddenly I couldn't bear the idea of more lawn mowers. I didn't know if I could bring Mother around on Dave, and I didn't know how much I wanted to. When he proposed, walking hand in hand with me around the quadrangle for the umpteenth time in our courtship, he'd kept it simple. No dinner, no knee, no ring. He took my face in his hands. I loved that; he was the first to do that, and I've loved it ever since. But I blushed red hot and told him I didn't know. I asked for time. I didn't know if I could handle being in his family but not *of* his family. I also figured Poppa would have defended him if he'd felt Dave was the one for me, and he hadn't. Poppa hadn't said a word.

The opportunity in Munich was a six-week position. A woman Mother's age from the Junior League, with whom I often did hospital visits, had an older brother who was in Munich working on a book, and his typist had come home due to a family emergency. He had a deadline, and he needed to finish. Could I type? Fortunately she didn't ask if I could type *fast*.

Six weeks in Germany. So I lay there, frightened of the unknown but maddened by the eternal lawn mowers of central Missouri, and decided that getting away was exactly what I needed. Getting away by marrying someone your parents mistrust isn't getting away at all. The parental presence is eternal. It's either benevolent or malevolent. You get to choose.

Mother never would have agreed to Munich if she hadn't been so afraid of feeling judged by Dave. She was worried about me, of course, but this time Poppa did step in. He took me with him to the hardware store on an errand one morning and he said to me, "Lillian, you're going to have to make your mother just a little bit happier with your arrangements in Germany, and then it'll all be fine." The writer, Mr. Jessop, had told his sister that I could take over his typist's room, as she had decided not to come back, but Poppa told me Mother didn't like that I'd be living alone.

"But it was okay for the other girl," I pouted, and he said, "And it'll be okay for you too. We're just going to have to tell a little fib."

"What kind of fib?"

"Well, can we not tell Mother that one of your Vassar girls is in Munich as well? And that you'll be able to stay with her?"

So I lied to Mother, and I lied to Dave. I told him it would be great for me to get some experience before coming back and talking about marriage, since I didn't feel I was bringing much to it. "Preparation is everything," I said.

He shook his beautiful head. Dave was no dummy. "Anyway," he said, "the fire has gone out of your kiss."

"Has it?" I said. "Was there fire in my kiss?"

"Not really," he said, which seemed unkind at the time, but in fact wasn't. Dave was honest and good. I was in for much, much unkinder partings.

God, that was so long ago. I remember crying at the airport, and I remember mixed feelings about everyone, everything. But transitions are so unclear.

I don't remember the last things I said to Dave, but I remember what I packed. I arrived in Munich in September 1956 with one suit. This one was beige, made of good cotton twill. The jacket had a belt, and the kind of pockets on the hip meant for slipping your fingers into when posing for photos. Change and tissues and train tickets fell out of them. All women's suits had skirts then. The skirts were below the knee, of course. And mine always were, anyway, even in the sixties. My legs are just too long to show that much of them.

On the
Importance of
Big Pockets

In those days you could wear the same outfit to work every day as long as it was presentable. I had to buy a second one, though, because I was cold. I hadn't realized how quickly fall comes on in that part of Europe. The one I bought in a shop near the office was dark green tweed. The jacket was shorter than the beige one, with heavy buttons that felt so good as I slid them through their buttonholes. They felt dependable, and hugged me securely inside. I had to have the sleeves let down, of course. The pockets on the jacket could accommodate my whole hand, and I discovered they were even big enough for the paperback copy of *The Brothers Karamazov* I had brought with me from the States. I also bought shoes. Good leather no-nonsense German lace-up shoes for walking the streets to work and back. I changed into my pumps when I arrived at Mr. Jessop's office in the morning. In the pumps I was six feet tall, and I loved it. I've never minded getting attention for my height, except from Mother. "For God's sake, put a necklace around that *thing*," she said to me once, as I was about to go out. She was referring to my neck.

At the end of each day I put the walking shoes on for the trip home and the four-story climb to my room, formerly a maid's quarters. Once there, I took some marks out of my bag and put them in one pocket, and put *The Brothers* into the other. Downstairs, a few doors along, was a small restaurant. I would order, then open the book. I felt small again in the evenings, and horribly self-conscious. I didn't stand out for my height in the evenings, but for my foreignness.

I suppose a few words of the unbelievably complicated novel went down with my schnitzel, but I can't say I'm sure I ever digested a full sentence. It never occurred to me to toss it and get a book that suited me better. I was supposed to have read it in college, and I was still trying. It was important to me to finish it. I will one day.

I would have gone insane if Mr. Jessop's office hadn't been in the bureau where he had formerly worked as a journalist. He was all work, and the monotony would have killed me. Being in the bureau gave me the chance to interact with the interesting people working around us. One of the girls who typed for the journalists, Sofia, invited me to a dinner party. Very informal, she said, but still, I had nothing to wear, only suits. I had no choice but to go back to the only shop I knew. Whatever I bought would require alterations, and I didn't have the time to look around in other shops in town. I'd seen other places on my weekend walks, but I couldn't remember where they were. I always meant to note them down when I got home, but I never did. And beyond not being able to imagine seeking them out, I couldn't imagine going into them. Every time I thought about entering a place where *The Brothers* couldn't protect me, I practically stopped breathing.

Bells rang when I opened the shop door and a stout *Frau* of about fifty appeared. She had a blond chignon, and up close a dark mustache as well. She wasn't the same woman from before. After a few moments she understood that it was best not to talk to me, and merely shadowed me with a helpful air as I looked at a few things on the racks. The one I finally pulled all the way out was navy blue grosgrain. "*Ja. Ja,*" she said, pumping her head. She took the dress from me and marched off to the fitting room, a door next to a set of three mirrors. "*Ja? Ja?*" she kept saying as I changed. I could get into the dress, but the fitting room didn't fit me at all. I'm sure she heard my elbows knocking the walls, my bottom jangling the old doorknob. When I came out, she looked at the dress on me and said, "Okay," taking me by the hips and pulling me into position in front of the mirrors. At first I couldn't really see the dress at all, just her hands, which were a man's hands although her short nails were painted a deep red. They first came around the front of my ribs to test the slack there, then tugged at the fit on my hips, then shot up to grab the fabric at my shoulders. Soon she was inserting pins here and there and here and there, and the dress took shape around me. The sleeves began right at my shoulder joint and went to my elbow. The neckline was low but showed no cleavage. The darts respected that my breasts are small but nonetheless present, especially when lifted. She lifted them decisively, pressing a hand on the skin above each one and pulling upward, placing them where they ought to go. The skirt was to the knee, straight. I looked like a candlestick, but I was used to that, ever since skirts became streamlined.

She put her firm hands on my hips and popped her head out from behind my shoulder. "*Schön?*" she asked.

"*Ja,*" I said. "*Schön. Ja. Danke.*"

She made it clear to me with the calendar that the dress would be ready the next evening.

Sofia picked me up in a taxi, wearing a very modern black-and-white dress, so we looked absolutely terrible together. One of us looked ridiculous, and I could only assume it was me, since these were her friends we were joining and she knew what was appropriate. Sure enough, all eyes were on me as we went through the open door at the top of the narrow stairs. I noticed the door was a beautiful buttercup yellow, and it reminded me of home, and then everyone looked at me and I blushed from the roots of my hair to the spaces between my toes, the way I always have. It was a full-body fever, especially because everyone was sitting at a long low table, looking at my thighs then up my nose.

Sofia introduced me to our host, Laszlo. He stood up and was over six feet, and Hungarian. His heavy hair hung in shiny waves, and his eyelashes sprang away from his blue eyes as if the color surprised them. His eyes weren't pale blue like George Junior's; they were more like lapis. He invited me to sit by him while Sofia plopped down elsewhere. I folded myself in three and sat, mostly on my right hip, leaning toward him. The wine we brought was opened. Finally there was some red flowing after the endless glasses of Liebfraumilch being poured all over town. Everyone spoke English for a few minutes, but when Laszlo passed me a plate of sliced salami and told me I was so beautiful I could be a Magyar princess, it was back to German for everyone but us. There was sour German bread, and boiled potatoes, big bowls of butter, olives, pickles, and wine, wine, wine. I found myself telling Laszlo about buttercups, and he got me a pen so I could draw one on a napkin. I knew I wouldn't be able to, but I tried because Laszlo's eyes were sparkling, even though it was a pretty napkin and a shame to spoil it. By this time I'd had to extend my legs under the table and a man and a woman having an intimate chat were leaning toward each other right over my feet. We were drinking our wine out of juice glasses. That was another reason I agreed to draw a buttercup. The normal rules didn't appear to apply. Nor did the artistic rules of proportion. I couldn't get it right. By the time we'd collapsed into giggles the napkin had a whole wacky garden on it, but not one buttercup. Laszlo invited me around again the following night and I said yes.

I left the party before Sofia. We waved across the room. The next day was Saturday, so I didn't get the chance to ask her if she'd be at Laszlo's again for dinner. They seemed like good friends; I just assumed she'd be there.

Nobody was, though. I guess I showed up around eight, and still the stairs were quiet and the buttercup door closed. There was no answer to my knock, but the handle turned, so I went in. There was only one lamp lit, as there had been the previous night, and the table was bare except for an unlit candle in a wine bottle and a heel of bread. My heart thumped so hard my ribs hurt. The insides of my cheeks were tingling. There was a sudden clattering and whistling on the stairs and I knew it was Laszlo. The whistling stopped and the clatter increased and I knew he had noticed the open door. I took a step behind it, as if that could possibly have interrupted what was without any doubt about to take place. I heard the sea in my ears.

I saw him first, as he looked around the room. His arms were full of groceries. When he finally found me, I felt the shock waves of the shudder that ran through his body. He half placed, half dropped the groceries on the floor and took the statue I had become into his arms, asking me questions, not waiting for answers, calling me Princess, licking my face. I remember his tongue better than I remember anything else.

Such things weren't called rape back then.

I ate bread and cheese in my room the next day after sleeping late and mending the blue dress. It hung quietly next to my suits in the narrow wardrobe. I didn't go out. On Monday, Sofia came to my desk wearing a huge smile.

"Just what you needed, am I right?" she said.

"Friday night was lovely, thank you," I said.

"Friday? Friday was just dinner. You get dinner every night. I'm talking about Saturday."

"Oh," I said, feeling the fever of my blush. I tried to tidy a few papers.

She waited, but nothing came out of my mouth. "Interesting," she said. "Welcome to Bohemia."

That night I put *The Brothers* in my pocket and went downstairs and ate sausages. This was decades ago now, but I remember that it was sausages because I stared at them for ages while my mind ran circles around what Sofia had said to me. *Just what you needed.* It was humiliating to think that she had pegged me so easily as a novice. And that Laszlo had imagined that I would come to him alone after only one meeting. But they were both right. In Europe it seemed people regularly knew you better than you knew yourself.

Mr. Jessop never learned the first thing about me, though. And he was the most boring interesting man who ever lived. I've never yawned so much in my life as I did in that little office, typing and typing, listening to him explain why he'd left something out or put something back in so ignore the cross-outs. There were times when his brown metal filing cabinet and he seemed interchangeable to me. Both were plain, both contained pure information, neither had character.

Still, my life hinges completely on that office. If it hadn't been located there, brown filing cabinet and all, then the magazine wouldn't have known about me, and wouldn't have picked me up as a secretary for the Paris bureau when my six weeks were through. I wouldn't have lived in Paris, and I wouldn't have met Willis. I wouldn't have moved to London, and I wouldn't have moved to New York. I wouldn't have met Ted.

On Behaving
Abroad, and
in General

So many people say that everything happens for a reason. I've always felt that things happen because the things before them happen, that's all. I met Willis because I wanted to sit in the sun, and that morning the sun was hitting the tables of a café that Willis passed on his way to buy a newspaper.

I met him the moment I became comfortable in France. I was sitting with a cup of coffee. In Paris, I didn't need *The Brothers*. Coffee kept me company. I was reflecting on how easy it had been to buy a new kettle, and he walked up to my table and practically shouted, "You're new. When'd you hit town, Slim?"

I blushed, but I kept my cool. I'd grown up a little in Germany. "Not that new," I said.

"New or not," he said, "welcome."

"Why did you assume I spoke English?" I asked.

"It's always worth a shot," he said, grinning. "Plus, no European woman would sit at a café with a kettle on the chair next to her." He picked the kettle up and sat himself down on the chair. For the duration of the conversation he held it on his lap. Every once in a while he tapped out a rhythm on it with his fingernails.

I've noticed this all over the world. There are foreigners who are aware they are guests in their adopted country, and there are others who behave like they're in a playground. This was Willis. He was a magazine photographer with an amazing eye for line, and he swept me up in his lanky, uncensored, Texan fun. He erased David. He eclipsed Laszlo. He shouted, he snorted, he roared, he applauded. He bought me a little Jaguar convertible from a friend who was leaving. It had been gently used, and it accepted my legs.

I bought myself a really attractive driving outfit. It had trousers a bit like jodhpurs, and a gray tweed jacket. I wore a cream silk scarf with it. It's a shame women have stopped tying a scarf around their heads for driving. With the right scarf, never a bandana of course, it looks so elegant. There's no dignity in tousled hair, and no one cares anymore. A bit of Grace Kelly was in all of us those days. I can't understand why we couldn't go through the sixties and free love and all that with our hair intact. I wore kaftans and I lit candles and I draped myself in beads, but I never saw the need not to do my hair. We're not cavewomen. Cavewomen don't drive.

Willis didn't give a damn about the Joneses. I wished I didn't. I still wish I didn't. I care mostly about the little things, though. I don't wear white after September. I don't serve ice cream after dinner unless the little tub is on a nice china plate. Even though I only ever make coffee in my Melitta, I still keep the silver coffee set that came to me when Poppa died on display on the sideboard. I hardly ever polish it, but it still looks right. It's important that it's there, where I can get to it if I want it. These things mean a lot to me. For the big things—what someone might call moral things, the fundamental life philosophy things—the Joneses had no part in that for me. Isn't that amazing? I can get so caught up in worrying about my hair, but the fact that the love of my life was a married man, that was no big deal. It was painful, but how society saw it didn't touch me. How my family saw it—how they chose not to like Ted—that hurt me. That hurt hugely. But the Joneses? No. Never. That's love, you see. You can't argue.

Part of Willis's attraction was his devil-may-care attitude. But when he asked me to dinner on the day we met, it wasn't his attitude that made me accept. It was the event—a gala reception for Henry and Clare Boothe Luce. She had recently become ambassador to Italy. Willis made a big deal about her illegitimate birth to a dancer, over the glasses of wine that he bought us to drink in the sun. Then he bought me a black satin dress. "Don't you dare wear a necklace," he told me when I stepped out of the dressing room to show him. Whatever happened between us in the next few years, I'll thank him for that as long as I live.

That was a lovely party. I felt scared and alive, and Willis started dozens of conversations for me. He'd leave me alone with people just long enough for a little chat, and then would drag me to meet someone else, in a pattern that became set in cement. Going to a party with him was exhausting. It was a crash course in socializing.

We traveled a lot too. One early summer, he had the task of photographing the three hundredth anniversary of a Provençal vineyard. We took the Jaguar, but Willis drove. Even in the passenger seat he drove, so it was easier to give him the wheel entirely. It was August, when the vineyards are green and the grapes are dark and round but not ready yet. We drove all day, leaving Paris in the cool of six a.m. People don't realize how quickly Paris surrenders to fields as you go south. It's almost immediate. And it's flat.

Willis was the kind of guy who shot out of bed like a rocket in the morning, and naturally he wanted to drive without stopping. I complained until he stopped in a village bar for coffee and a pee, and I found out where we could get bread. I'd brought cheese and sliced ham, and tomatoes to eat like apples; he'd brought wine.

I never tire of the wind when driving, and I love the amazement you feel that it's suddenly so peaceful when you stop. I hope that is what death is like. Peaceful when you stop.

We drove for hours and hours. Willis didn't want to consult a map; he was sure he could find the place, not too far from Cassis. It was probably after two when we stopped to eat, by which time the cheese was perfectly soft. The wine cut it perfectly. Willis knew what he was doing with wine. He hadn't studied, but his arms just seemed to reach for the right bottle. We were sitting on a low hill, facing away from the road and toward a yellow valley. "I've got half a mind to take you right here in the grass," Willis said.

I looked at him. "You talk like that and still expect me to introduce you to my parents?"

"Come on, kiddo," he said. "Your daddy must have taken Mother in the grass a time or two. If his life's been worth living at all."

The image was so ridiculous I laughed. Willis laughed too, and bit me on the neck. Once we were in the car again I kept thinking about it, though. It was impossible to imagine Mother and Poppa in the grass. She demanded a more

distant form of homage. But what kept me thinking was
the idea that Poppa may have had someone else in the grass
at some point in his life. Maybe in France. Maybe during
the war. He would have been so good at it, so considerate.
He would have made an effort to make sure her clothes
didn't get dirty, her skin didn't get pricked or stung. He was
a charming Midwestern man, and I started to get angry
that Mother denied him this simple pleasure.

We arrived at our hotel in the late afternoon. The sun
was strong but it was cool in the shade of the buildings.
Willis parked around behind the hotel and propped the
bonnet open so the poor car could cool down. I walked
around the sand-colored stone building and looked at the
little wildflowers growing here and there in the grass beyond the parking lot. "Go on in," Willis shouted over at
me, but I shook my head and pretended to be really interested in the flora. I just couldn't walk up the front steps and
sign a lie into their guestbook. He always wanted me to
push the boundaries. Sometimes what he felt was a playground was more of a gauntlet for me. So I waited. He
signed us in as "M. et Mme. Willis Long" and we sat down
in the restaurant for an early dinner. Another thing I like
about driving is that whatever you eat when you've finished

a long journey tastes fantastic. I don't think I've ever enjoyed a green salad so much. We started with that and ate at least another course if not two, but the salad is all I can remember.

Now I've learned to travel with everything I could possibly need, but back then I kept getting caught unprepared. There was the time we went to Monaco so Willis could photograph the royal family, and we were invited to a reception, and I had to buy gloves. I didn't know that gloves had to be two inches above the elbow for shaking royal hands. At that time, the fashion was for evening gloves to be cut a few inches *below* the elbow, so I bought those. Everyone else's gloves were longer than mine. I was trembling as we approached Princess Grace. All I could think of to do was to keep my elbows tight against my ribs, so that she wouldn't notice the breach of protocol. I must have looked horribly malformed. She was wonderful, though. So warm, even though she really did look like porcelain. It was hard to think of her as real, but then you looked at Rainier's ears, and you knew she had to be. As long as one of them looked like a normal person, you knew they both were.

This time, we were invited to have dinner with the owner of the vineyard—a count—and his friends. I hadn't even considered the possibility. I wouldn't presume. I had my driving suit, a white blouse, and a cotton sweater; that was it. The only boutiques were miles away, and there wasn't time. I didn't want to accept. Willis insisted. "Imagine turning this guy down!" he said. "God."

"Imagine showing up for dinner in *tweed*," I said back. He didn't understand anything.

"We could go as twins in matching white shirts," he said.

"Ha," I said. "Even tweed is less offensive than clowning."

"Tweed it is, then," he said, and shot me with his fingers. "Gotcha."

I had spent the day reading and strolling, and had to wipe the vineyard dust off my shoes. I did what I could with my hair, and put my eyeliner on very, very carefully.

The stone of the château gave off the accumulated warmth of the long summer day. We were greeted at the door by a butler, and Willis slapped him on the back as if they were old pals. I wasn't sure I knew how to behave, but I knew absolutely that Willis *didn't*. The valet escorted us along smooth stone floors, between cool stone walls. I was painfully aware that my comfortable flat shoes weren't making the *tip-tap* sound of a woman on her way to an elegant dinner, and then we were ushered into a large room full of people and flowers. The evening sun reached straight in through the windows and made everyone look healthy and content. The windows looked down over the vineyards toward the village. A fine-boned older man in a double-breasted jacket, open-necked shirt and cravat turned to welcome us. He looked like David Niven. His smile was so large he must have found us very amusing. *"Enchanté,"* he said, and so did I, and Willis slapped him too. Then Willis recognized someone, and strode over to greet him. The count took my elbow and guided me to a linen-covered bar by the cold fireplace.

"I'm so sorry about my clothes, Monsieur le Comte," I said.

"Henri," he said, "please," and passed me a glass of his rosé.

"Delicious!" I blurted, sounding as if I were surprised.

He laughed. Of course I blushed. I wanted to apologize but I couldn't form words. Putting down his own glass, the count asked me if I'd do him the honor of sitting next to him at the meal. He made a sign to the valet, who immediately opened the doors in the far end of the room, and took my elbow again.

The dining room was exactly as I would have imagined

the dining room of a French château. I checked off everything on my mental list: white linen, crystal glasses, silver cutlery, dark wood, wall hangings. Add to this half a dozen crystal vases of white roses and lavender placed every few feet along the immense table. We were eighteen for dinner. We arranged ourselves and sat. Willis was on the opposite side, farther down, between two women of a certain age. The sun was coming straight in through the windows, and I could feel the sweat trickling from my underarms into my bra.

Gentlemen ask you questions about yourself and look like they find the answer very interesting. When I told the count what I did, he said, "A fine assistant is a precious thing." He asked about the magazine's methods for gathering news from behind the Iron Curtain. I certainly didn't know much, but I talked anyway. He continued listening actively, then said, "Don't worry. It will come up, the curtain. They will miss our wine too much."

"Oh," I said, "I'm sure those who drank it before are still drinking it now."

"Precisely," he said.

By this time we were eating lobster. A pair of white-gloved hands kept appearing between us and replacing the previous course's plate with a clean one before I'd had time to finish. On the other side, another pair of gloves expertly served the next course between two large spoons. I wanted to eat but I was struggling. Between talking and enjoying the wine I couldn't really apply myself to the food, and then they took it away. I noticed the count didn't finish anything either, but where it may be elegant in a host I felt sure it was offensive in a guest. My napkin was covered in lipstick and upper-lip sweat.

And then the waiters came in with sorbet, little glass bowls of sorbet arranged in a circle around the decorative tops of pineapples. Each of us received one, and a pretty glass of calvados as well.

The count was talking to me as I looked down at my spoon, wondering if I could force myself to pick it up.

"This is what we call a *trou normand*," he said. "A Norman hole. It's something to clean the palate between very different courses. Traditionally it should be an apple sorbet, but I adore pineapple. Please." He indicated that I should go ahead and taste it.

I hate pineapple so much, it might as well have been a delicate serving of blood and hair. I tried to smile but it made my lip tremble. I looked at Willis, desperate for him to recognize my predicament and get on his white horse, but he was deep into some tall tale and had too much of a head of steam to switch tracks.

He looked so happy. Stalling was my only option. "Please go ahead, Henri. I must excuse myself for a moment to use *les toilettes.*"

"Of course, of course," he said, standing, signaling to the valet. "Take your time." God knows I would. I'd stay long enough for the sorbet to melt.

The toilet was clearly designed for ladies, and quite recently. Maybe there weren't any toilets on the ground floor originally. Maybe upstairs they were still connected to high cisterns and flushed with a long chain. I would have loved to creep up the stairs and look around, but there was the question of the valet. This toilet was modern, in a room with a tiled counter inset with a pretty porcelain sink. I could breathe in there, although the mirror showed me terrible things. I had known my lipstick would be gone, but I hadn't anticipated that the nervous sweating I was doing would have begun to curl my hair. I looked mortifyingly Midwestern, but in my haste to leave the dining room I had left my handbag on my chair. So stupid. Stupid, stupid, stupid. I made sure the door was locked, took off my jacket and camisole, and splashed my neck, chest, and underarms with the extremely cold water that came out of the tap. It felt so good I did it again. I wet a corner of a linen hand towel and dabbed at my face. I decided that if I messed up my eyeliner I'd leave the château immediately, but I did okay. Before putting my clothes back on, I flapped them smartly to dispel the smell of distress. There was nothing to do about the curls, but I ran my fingers carefully through my hair so at least they would curl in the same direction.

When I finally emerged, the unsmiling valet appeared from around a corner. I felt I'd never experienced anything more discreet in my life. He showed me back to the dining room. The count stood, I sat, then he sat. The pineapple was gone. Cheese and grapes now dominated the table.

I said, "Wow!" and the count laughed. I took a sip of calvados, which was pure fire in my throat. I pretended the coughing was brought on by the laughter.

In bed that night, Willis said, "Sure you're satisfied with the likes of me?"

It was an excellent question, but I had no idea why he asked it. It wasn't his style at all.

"Why?"

"Because you could be having yourself a count."

"What?"

"He was yours for the taking, babe."

"He was not."

"Ripe for the plucking."

"He was *not*. You just don't know a gentleman when you see one," I told him. Then I thought for a while, blinking at the dark ceiling, replaying the event. I decided Willis was mistaken. Willis really, really didn't understand anything.

On English

as a Foreign

Language

Of course my parents had a bit of trouble swallowing Willis. Among other things.

On the first day of their first and only trip to visit me in Paris, I walked into their hotel dining room to find Mother shocked and disgusted. I have to say she looked otherwise handsome, but her face was pinched with discomfort and I thought, *Oh God, it's only the first day, please let this be something we can get over quickly.* There are so many confusing feelings involved in entertaining Midwestern parents in a European city. I suppose I'd been in Europe too long to remember that not everyone in the world hankered to start the day with a croissant. No matter where they were, Mother and Poppa asked for sweet rolls for breakfast in hotels. It was nearly lunchtime already, but they still insisted on starting the day the usual way. Apparently when they asked for sweet rolls they had received blank looks and had rightly understood that the word "roll" was the culprit, so tried asking for sweet *bread* instead. I arrived just after the waiter had taken the lid off the thymus gland of a calf.

Mother said, "Calf's *thymus*, Lillian? I wish I weren't too tired and hungry to laugh."

"Well, you could try it, since it's here now."

"Don't push her, Lil," Poppa said, squeezing my elbow.

Impasse. So I said I'd eat it. I waved a waiter over and ordered Mother a selection of pastries, and I ate the sweetbreads, pretending not to mind in the slightest. They tasted a bit like bacon, so I told Mother they tasted a lot like bacon. I added that I'd heard that sweetbreads of pancreas rather than thymus were said to be more delicious. She laughed at that, and it was nice to see.

After we finished eating, Mother pulled out her cigarettes and I surprised them both by pulling out mine. Poppa didn't miss a beat, though, and lit them for each of us, Mother first, of course, and went back to his coffee, smiling at the spring sun coming through the windows. Mother and I puffed. I didn't want a cigarette; I wanted some orange juice, but instead I built a smoke tower to rival hers. Smoking is only convivial if you partake of the same pack; otherwise it's territorial.

I knew very little about Mother then. I still don't have the facts straight. She wouldn't tell anyone what year she was born because she was a year older than Poppa. She had been a rural teacher before marriage and the suburbs, but showed no teacherly tendencies at any point in my life with her. She had two charming sisters who irritated her but nonetheless kept her secrets. Her drink was bourbon on the rocks. Sitting across from her in the hotel that morning, though, what I did or didn't know about her and what I did and didn't like about her didn't matter. I wanted my parents to have a good time, and I wanted to show them what a big girl I was, and I wasn't sure how to work it all out. Then it hit me like my own private earthquake that Mother and I were wearing the same shade of dark red nail polish. I put out my half-smoked cigarette and tucked my hands under my thighs.

"So," I said in my high school voice, "what do you want to do today?" They visibly relaxed. It's unfortunate how we have to cripple ourselves for love, but it's a fact. We have to. Poppa did that more elegantly than any human I've ever met, keeping his thoughts to himself on Mother's complaints and desires, giving the impression that he had gained rather than lost something as a result.

I can't remember where I took them that day. Probably the Arc de Triomphe and the Champs-Élysées. That would have made sense. I know we had beautiful weather. I remember our nail polish flashing in the sun. For dinner with my parents and Willis, I changed shades. He would have remarked upon the matching fingernails. *The clothes-horse doesn't fall far from the tree, now, does it?* he'd have hooted. I took off the red and put on an extremely dark plum after my bath, knowing it would look as good with the black-and-white satin dress as the red, and sat naked on the edge of the bed waiting for it to dry. Willis took a photo. When he couldn't keep his hands to himself any longer, he pushed me onto my back and took me. I kept my hands in the air, away from our bodies. That was fun. It was fun to think of when we walked into the hotel bar and greeted Mother. Less fun to think of when I hugged Poppa, though, and when I introduced him to Willis.

Willis ordered drinks and commandeered the conversation. He was just back from Naples, where he believed not only that every other person he met was a Mafioso but also that they were now his best friends. I drank and cringed and watched my parents' reactions. Mother smoked and accepted another drink and asked Willis about his people in Texas. Willis was succinct for once. Poppa stuck with two drinks and nodded. Willis turned to Poppa and said, "You saw some of the first war here in France, Lil tells me."

"Well, yes, I suppose I did," Poppa answered.

"You suppose, huh?" Willis said, ready to laugh, but he caught my look. "Well," he said, and took a swig of his gin.

"Paris has a brand-new face on these days anyway. It's not the same town you liberated, George. No, sir. You'll see that. We're back to flowers and smooches in the street now, aren't we, Lil?"

"Hallelujah," I said, and raised my glass. Willis and Poppa and then Mother followed suit.

"To smooches," Willis said.

Mother and Poppa hesitated—it wasn't their sort of word—so I said it, "To smooches," and we drank.

At dinner, Mother talked about the trip she and Poppa had taken to Florida two months before to visit her sister Celia, and how Celia's husband had spent so much time tending his hunting dogs that she wondered why Celia didn't come back to Missouri, and Poppa said he supposed she enjoyed the beautiful sunsets over the lake. Mother said, "Celia?" but I knew Poppa was saying that he had been touched by that evening light.

For all Willis's brutal directness, I knew that he would have loved the Florida sunsets too. I also knew that it would be hard to convince anyone that this was true. People say it shouldn't matter, that you shouldn't worry about whether or not other people see your lover the way you do, but when are things ever that simple? Have the people who say that lived at *all*?

I spent a lot of money telling all this to Alma years later in New York, when the strain of loving Ted, and waiting for Ted, and enduring the disapproval of the family got too great. Alma smoked while I talked and cried. It's a shame shrinks can't smoke in their own offices anymore. The smoke looked like her thoughts. Shrinks who just listen make me nervous. We entered areas of feeling that I worried might overwhelm me completely. Hate, for example. It's an emotion I continue to avoid, both in myself and in others, but I like to encourage others to admit to it if they can. I like to watch when they do. I now prefer women who breathe fire when truly provoked to those who sit alone in their bedrooms and cry. Back then, though, I was still convinced that hate wasn't allowed, and that crying was the only path to peace. As I told Alma my stories, my crying led not to relief but to more crying. The well felt bottomless. Standing at the door after an early session, knowing there was someone in the waiting room who deserved his or her turn, I couldn't get myself to leave. Alma asked me if I'd like to come more than once a week for a while.

"Yes, please," I blubbed.

"That's okay. We'll do that," she told me.

This still didn't get me out.

"Would you like to come every day?" She was smiling.

"Yes, please." I meant it. Still I stood.

"Would you like to move in?"

Now I laughed, which released me. I felt really stupid, but I could finally walk through the door, and, more importantly, back out into New York and my life. My life with Ted but not with Ted, with, without, with *and* without. Alma said that would keep until we'd talked about Mother, and Poppa, even George Junior, which was weird, and Vassar. She made a joke to get me back out on the street, but out there I cried again. Once even, actually maybe twice, on my way home, I imagined coming across a sharp rock protruding from the sidewalk and deliberately falling so that it pierced my temple and killed me, but of course there never was one. Also, Alma had tried to convince me that even though I felt each time I saw her that I was descending deeper into a dark, rank pit, I was actually climbing a ladder out of it.

On Remodeling

ichael likes tea in the morning, and I always wish I could have a steaming pot waiting for him when he comes into the kitchen, but it's impossible to time it correctly. I sat at the little table for a while after I finished my breakfast and wondered what to do about the corner cabinet. I can't just keep putting Scotch tape on it to keep it closed. Well, I can. But there must be something else I can do. Maybe a sliver of cardboard in the hinge. People who ask me why I don't just replace the old cabinets don't understand at all. When you choose new kitchen cabinets you don't just choose new cabinets. You set off an avalanche of decisions to be made: Will they clash with the countertop? Will I hate the way the handles stick out? Will having new cabinets make the old fridge look too shabby? I keep meaning to have some gay friends over to ask their opinions.

I like to think that if Mother had been born a bit later and in more cosmopolitan circumstances, she would have had gay friends. She would have had a good laugh with them, maybe even a good, wicked laugh. They would have enjoyed her well-made dress suits, and maybe they would have improved her taste in interiors.

She had a decorator over once, when I had just finished college and was volunteering here and there. This woman looked around the house at all the details—the things that couldn't be reupholstered or painted over, the paintings. She came last to my room and pointed at the little Zao Wou-ki watercolor I had just bought. "Well," she said, "that's the only art of any value here." I saw Mother stiffen.

It didn't go with my ice-blue room at all. I had leaned it up against the wall in anticipation of living somewhere else. I still do that. I buy stuff for future walls. Fantasy walls. This was the first, though. I'd seen the painting in the window of a little gallery in St. Louis, and started going in to stare at it after my activities with the Junior League nearby. I had volunteered to read to children in a hospital in the city, which I adored. Afterward, someone from the Junior League would drive me to the bus station. But first I went into the gallery. I couldn't walk by it; I had to go in. If this has happened to you, you know what I mean. Time stops. You don't feel your body, just the swirl behind your eyes. Finally the woman in the shop asked me how much I felt I could pay, as it was obvious to her I was blocked by my budget. I floundered. After a moment she very elegantly suggested an installment plan. I would bring her ten dollars as regularly as possible, and she would leave the painting up with a little SOLD sign beside it. "Good for you, good for me," she said, explaining how SOLD signs always got hesitant browsers' juices flowing. So eventually I had it, a little watercolor window on my future propped up against the wall of my bedroom, and Mother had to eat crow, because she had said it was very strange and the decorator had called it valuable.

I can admit that I now need a decorator. I know this kitchen is ridiculous. Not enough space to swing a cat. Between the sink and the oven there's no space to swing even a mouse. Silly. But no one's offered a solution that feels right. I should see the design and time should stop. You should know it's the one for you.

That was Ted. The first time I saw him I knew, and it wasn't just how he looked; it was the energy that came off him. I felt it coming out of his eyes but also off his forearms when he rolled up his starched sleeves. It was in the shine on his eyebrow hairs and in the deep creases on the tops of his gleaming shoes. I felt it in the way his trousers slid along his long calves when he walked.

It was August 15, 1968. I was thirty-five. We knew that the new managing director would be moving into the New

York office that day. Those of us who were interested had read his bio, and some people in the office had met him when he was with AP. Most of the assistants hadn't thought too much about him, but I was going to be his PA. I read the bio. I asked around. He'd attended the School of Journalism at Indiana University. He also had a law degree. He'd worked for newspapers in Pennsylvania and California before joining AP, where he progressed from reporter to editor. He had a wife and three children. He was fifty-one, and, as I noticed when he walked across the outer office to where I was standing by my desk, he limped.

He limped, but he did so as if he'd always limped and that was the normal way, when in fact he'd been wounded in the war, before most of our boys even had a chance to be. It was months and months before he was willing to tell me, actually. We could only snatch short moments alone for ages, but there was finally a trip, a hotel, a chance to sleep and wake up and see his skin against white sheets. I traced the scars on his thigh, just above his knee.

"France?" I said, watching my fingers.

His hair shushed against the pillow as he shook his head no. "Libya," he said.

"Were you there for long?"

"Not long enough. Went in August, back home for Christmas. Nineteen forty."

My sleepy mind ticked over. "Nineteen forty?"

"That's what I said."

"But we didn't enter the war until nineteen forty-one, right?"

"That's right."

I tipped my head back to look into his face, and he was smiling at me. "Speak," I said. He just looked down at my hand on his knee. I pushed him with my body to shake the words out of him. "Speak," I said. "Speak now, or forever hold your ears to block out the nagging."

When he decided to talk, he pulled me to him so that his chin rested on my head and my right ear was suctioned against his neck. It's awkward to try and listen like that, with your neck twisted that far and only one ear available, but I didn't dare move. That's how he wanted to tell me, so that's how I'd be told.

"I enlisted with the British, before we entered the war," he said. "Rifle battalion."

He didn't say anything for a while, but kept me held against him, so I figured he wasn't finished. I tried to imagine what he was seeing. "Bayonets?"

"Yes."

"It's hard to imagine. Like you were fighting in the Boer War, or something."

"They were very important."

"But you have to get so close to use them."

He nodded against my head. "You save ammunition, though."

"But what if they have guns? I mean, who can you actually get close to without being killed first?"

"Sometimes you got close under cover of smoke. Sometimes you came across soldiers manning mortar, all spread out. I don't know why they weren't better armed."

"You stabbed them."

"If you could."

We were quiet for a moment. I felt like the room wasn't attached to a hotel anymore. It was just our minds. It was the inside of our minds.

"And did *you* stab people?"

He nodded against my head and I felt him waiting, like he didn't know how I'd feel about that, so I pulled him closer against me with the hand I'd been touching his scars with, the hand I wasn't lying on. I wanted to press my lips against his neck, but that would mean pulling my head away a bit, and I didn't want him to feel any separation between us at that moment, so I just waited. When he didn't say anything, I said, "Did people stab you?"

"No."

"So what got you in the leg?"

"Shrapnel."

Now I nodded, and my ear popped away from his neck, which was a relief, and since we were talking about the wound I felt I could look at it again. I went up on one elbow and leaned over toward it. "Did they need to reset the bone?"

"Yes, lots of it."

"And did they do that in Libya?"

"Yes."

"In a field hospital?"

"Those were in France. Ours were called desert hospitals."

I was about to ask another question, because it seemed that was what I had to do, but he said, "You know what I remember most vividly from that hospital? There were creases in the pillowcase. I was in pain when they brought me in. They'd bandaged me up before transporting me, but they hadn't had anything to deaden that kind of pain, so I wasn't clear in my head. I don't remember who was holding the stretcher, anything like that, but when they lifted me up and I looked at the cot I'd be transferred to, even as they tipped me onto it, I noticed the creases in the pillowcase, and it was everything I could do not to cry. You get used to things being dusty and gritty and oily. You really do. But then when there's something clean, something that's been folded carefully, and unfolded carefully, and it's there for your head, it's like your heart, it's like, I don't know. I can't describe it."

I wished he could. I wished I could have been the one to hear exactly what happened to his heart that day. But I didn't push him.

"Did you receive a Purple Heart?" I asked after a bit.

"No."

"Why not?"

"I was with the British, remember?"

"Oh yes. So did they give you anything, or just a clean pillowcase?"

"The Military Cross."

"For being wounded?"

He cleared his throat. "For gallantry, actually. I think it was 'exemplary gallantry.'"

I looked at his face again, and he shrugged. "No idea what for," he said. "It came as a surprise."

"No."

"I'm not lying."

"I still don't believe you."

"Suit yourself."

I thought for a second. "Maybe they thought it was gallant that a Yank signed up to help." I put on an English accent. "Jolly good show, soldier."

He laughed. "Maybe. Come here. I'll show you a jolly good show."

"Oh yeah?" I said. "I'll show you exemplary gallantry."

So you see? You see how right he was? You see how the design was just right? And how Willis and I weren't just right? Willis bought me beautiful clothes and took me beautiful places, but he got angry and said crazy stuff and was embarrassing when behavior mattered. I tried to imagine marrying him, but the idea was ridiculous. He would have been fun at the reception but a nightmare at the ceremony.

The transfer to London saved me. I remember packing, stuffing my suitcases with the clothes he'd given me. I even had to buy some webbing to tie them shut with. And then unpacking everything, and all of it looking so out of place in my dowdy little tenement.

When he came over to England to ask me to reconsider, the familiarity I felt when I was with him paled in comparison to the relief I felt at having the Channel between us. Actually, the familiarity had simply paled, even without the comparison. It didn't take long. When you're in a relationship you mold yourself to it. You curve your body around it and you curve your mind around it, in order to maintain it. Sometimes you don't realize you're crippled until it's too late.

That's not how I worded it to myself back then, of course. I was so unclear on things. But my heart was tender, and I knew that he chafed it.

We had dinner when he came over to London, and he looked different to me. I knew all the clothes he was wearing, and his hair was still the same, neatly trimmed, lightly oiled, as always belying his interior volcano. But he was no longer someone I adapted to. I chattered about my new job for a while, fiddling with my bread, until he couldn't stand it.

"Your new boss handsome?" he finally asked.

"Not especially," I said.

"Uh-huh," he said, and stretched a leg out to the side and looked at it.

We didn't talk or eat much after that. On the walk back to where I was staying it pained me so much that I had caused such a noisy man to fall silent. I wanted to put my hand on his shoulder, or on his heart. But of course I didn't reach out to him. If you touch them, it means they are allowed to touch you, and if he had touched me I would have screamed.

I was staying temporarily in what the English call a bedsit. It was on the second floor of a drab terrace house and had its own door at street level. I left Willis at the bottom of the stairs and turned at the top. He still had his hand on the door, keeping it open.

"Sure?" he said, after a moment.

I nodded. After another moment he let the door close and left.

I don't want that to happen with this kitchen. I don't want that horrible, exhausting confusion of moving away from the old but being unclear about the new. I want to see a design, and I want to *know*, because in my experience the new has been an extremely mixed bag.

On the

Food of

Love

J ohn, for example. My first beau in London after my transfer there. The relationship lasted less than two years, but I had to try so hard in that short time that it felt like much longer.

He had an unusually sweet singing voice, and favored Italian art songs and Henry Purcell. Particularly Purcell in the morning, and particularly the charming one that goes, *"If music be the food of love sing on, sing on, sing on, sing on till I am fill'd, am fill'd with joy."* His voice rang like bells against the bathroom tile.

Food is the food of love, though, not music. I've known that ever since Mary spoiled me with snacks between meals. Ever since Laszlo came up the stairs with his arms around a bag of groceries before throwing his arms around me instead. So when it came to interacting with John's two little children, I cooked.

When I arrived in Munich I couldn't boil an egg, and in Paris I bought pâté and cheese and salad and bread and that was dinner. London requires one to cook, so I took myself to Le Cordon Bleu and studied under the very severe

Monsieur Hervé, who was totally unromantic in his approach to cooking. As a result we joked among ourselves that he was either Belgian or more likely Swiss rather than French. He taught us the many ways to present the glory of the egg. He enlightened us on other topics as well, of course, but for some reason the egg represented the most meaningful part of my Cordon Bleu education. Maybe because until then it had always been a simple breakfast with salt and pepper, a garnish, or a last resort when the cupboard was otherwise bare. Over a few weeks it became a showstopper.

There was a party one night at the Highgate home of one of John's journalist friends. John picked me up at my apartment on his way there. Checked shirt and cuff links, as usual. It was a Friday night, and he had the children as he did every other weekend, so we brought them along. I put them to bed in a guest room and read them *Goodnight Moon*. That book was impossible to find in London, so I'd asked George Junior to send a copy over. I felt extremely glamorous in my silk and pearls, feminine and good, sitting in the guest room of an elegant London home reading to a pair of pretty children. When I returned to the living room the air was full of cigar smoke and the conversation was being dominated by a square-headed American gesticulating with the cut-crystal tumbler of Scotch in his fist. "Oh good, you're back," he said, and I felt a blast of hot prickles on my skin. "You can help us muddle something out."

"Well, I'll try," I said, perching on the arm of John's chair for moral support.

"You must have some of the inside poop on the USSR."

I said I wasn't very close to the source. I was secretary to the bureau chief at a weekly magazine in London, not a journalist in Berlin. Everyone was looking at me and my heart was pounding wildly.

"Lots in the magazine about Khrushchev lately," he said, trying to prompt me.

"Well," I said.

"Aha! I *knew* it," the guy said, bringing his drink down on the arm of his chair and leaving a splash of Scotch on the fabric.

"Knew what?" I asked, then wanted to kick myself for sounding thick.

"Khrushchev's days are numbered."

"I only said 'Well.'"

"You hesitated."

"I suppose anything's possible," John said, in a way that was slightly mocking.

"Oh no, you mark my words, John," the man said. "This is how they function."

"Excuse me," I said, getting up, and hoped they imagined that I needed the restroom. I went back to the guest room, where the children were sleeping, and closed the door behind me. Once I had sat down in the dark at the foot of one of the beds and had stopped hearing the sea in my ears, I was able to listen to the two of them breathing. My eyes adjusted to the dark. Marcus, the seven-year-old, breathed evenly in the bed I was sitting on. Mariana was dreaming energetically in the other. She would have been four then. I was calming down, but now I was worried about how to go back out to the party. I couldn't answer that question. I could only sit there and worry.

Eventually the door opened and John looked in. He could see me in the triangle of light from the hall. I was too embarrassed to look at him.

"Would you like to go home, Lillian?"

I nodded.

"Would you like to go home to *my* home, Lillian?"

Now I looked at him. I'd never stayed the night when his kids were with him before. Tears of love and relief came to my eyes, but I knew better than to throw my arms around him. True gentlemen are so often maladroit, and mustn't be toppled over. I just nodded again, and he nodded back. "I'll get your coat," he said.

When we got to John's and had transferred the children from our shoulders to their beds, all I wanted to do was cook. I was so happy. Dinner had been a strange bachelor effort, and we were both hungry, and John had eggs in the fridge.

After I had moved in completely and was cooking regularly, John became more and more frustrated with my attention to detail. "Oh, just make them some *toast*, for God's sake, Lillian! They're *hungry*!" he'd hiss at me while I was mashing young carrots into new potatoes or salting and rinsing cucumber spears to be wrapped in ham. "Why are you being so *tasteful*?" he cried once. "Children *have* no taste!"

"But they love what I cook," I bleated back.

"Anyone would love it if they'd been waiting for hours to have it on their plate," he said with his hands on his narrow hips. But the idea of opening a can of baked beans for them for speed's sake made my stomach lurch. To please John I'd sometimes give them canned tomato soup, but I'd console myself by making the croutons from scratch.

That night, though, after leaving the party early, coming home to John's with the children for the first time, I took all the time I wanted assembling a beautiful improvised frittata and a tomato vinaigrette. I remember holding each egg in my hand before I broke it into the bowl, appreciating its perfection. No other food offers that feeling of peace before you cook it, no other shell or rind so delicately protects so many options. I cooked slowly, and John waited quietly, and we sat and looked at each other across our plates and glasses and ate the love I'd made.

On Leaving
in Order to Stay

Living with John was like that Robert Frost poem about whether the world will end in fire or in ice and which is worse. He was so cold sometimes. He would go for days without speaking. He never seemed to have trouble finding the words for his foreign policy column, but speaking to me was often beyond him. I thought this was deep. To stupid me, it was part of his elegance.

It's so painful to be a disappointment when you're trying your best all the time. I never came home from work and merely put my feet up. I never went out without dressing carefully. I stayed up until all hours to get the dishes clean after an evening. I ran all over town for birthday gifts for the children, and he'd say, "Why do you waste your time like that, Lillian? Don't you have better things to do?" Men tell you they say things like this because they love you. So do mothers. That this doesn't feel like love to you surprises them.

As does your infidelity.

It all started with tango music in a restaurant. It made me feel sexy, but our chat over dinner was incredibly banal.

I tried to keep the energy up, but John was desultory. He was so intelligent, but this was a period during which he didn't want to talk about work. The evening was odd from the start. The walls were green. The music writhed into my blood like a hot oiled snake. I looked at John's neat hair, his shining cuff links, the beautiful mole at the corner of his mouth. The conversation was little better than gossip. I'm sure at some point I wondered deep down how long such a ridiculous dinner could possibly last. Then I heard a clattering of cutlery and felt the breeze as a large man rushed over to John from somewhere behind me. He made an effort to hide his face from me as he announced, "You are having dinner with the most, most beautiful woman in the world." Then he left the restaurant, but I had recognized his hands, his hair. Laszlo. Laszlo was in London. I was in London. John was ice. When Laszlo put two and two together and called the London bureau, I was ready to be found. I agreed to meet him for tea in the afternoon.

The tables in the tea shop were tiny, and after he indented both my cheeks with his velvet lips and left my skin tingling from the swipe of surrounding stubble, we sat, and our long legs interlocked under the table. I scooted my chair back and crossed my legs, but he stayed right where he was for a long moment. Then he leaned forward with his elbows on the table, and said, "Oh my God, Lillian, your *beautiful nostrils.*" When a man says something like this, you either suddenly remember an important meeting or you stay where you are in the heat of his curly-fringed eyes and indulge the idea of allowing him to enjoy your body.

The following weekend John took the children to see his parents. It was Easter. Laszlo and I heard church bells all morning. They made me sing. *"'Oranges and lemons,' say the bells of St. Clement's."* In his current mood, John wouldn't have laughed. Then again, I wouldn't have sung. When John got quiet, I got quiet. It was contagious. *"'You owe me five farthings,' say the bells of St. Martin's."* Laszlo guffawed and rubbed his stiff morning beard into my neck, and pushed me on my side to continue down my back, and scraped my inner thighs mercilessly, giggling and licking and then ripping me in two.

John didn't have much of an eye for changes in physical detail. Once I said to him, during tea with the children, "I think I'll go back to my old hairstyle." John said, "Which was . . . what?" Little Mariana said, "Can I come too?" So John didn't notice the abrasions. He did, however, get home earlier than I did a few weeks later to pack for a trip to Brussels and open a steamy letter from Laszlo. I was closing the front door saying, "Hiya, honey," as he walked toward me down the front hall. His eyes were rimmed in red. I asked him what was wrong and he took the sleeve of my jacket between two of his fingers as if I were something foul he'd found on the carpet. He led me into the kitchen, where Laszlo's letter was open on the table. Florid writing, impossible not to recognize. I didn't need to read it. The atmosphere around John was electric. He was visibly shaking with a shock and humiliation that inflamed my pity.

"Are you going to make some important decisions here or am I going to have to make them for you?" he asked.

"No," I said, straightening up. "I will." I felt great with Laszlo, but of course I didn't feel *good*.

"Okay then," he said, and went to Brussels.

Our living room was quite long, with doors that opened onto the tiny garden spanning the long wall. A four-seater couch faced the windows, and a love seat sat at a right angle to it under the window at the end. I was doing a crossword on the love seat when John came back from his trip. He hadn't called at all while he was away, and I didn't get up, just looked up from the paper. It's a terrible moment for any woman when her man, hitherto clean-cut, professionally respected, runs his hands through his hair and leaves it sticking up like a child after a nap. Then it gets worse. He starts talking. "Why not me, Lillian? Those things he wrote that you did together. Why not me?"

There's a place in Saint John on the eastern coast of Canada I once went to from Vassar. It's called Reversing Falls. A river flows into the Bay of Fundy there, but the tide comes in so forcefully that it pushes the river back up its course. There's a deep churning and mingling, but the tide wins for a while. This was me. I wanted to leave the room, but I didn't.

One of the most useful things I've learned in my life is that I can have an out-of-body experience when I need to. It's incredibly silly to me when people find it amazing, proof of life after death et cetera, that some people have watched themselves being operated on, particularly after a near-fatal accident. Has no one ever made the connection between them and victims of abuse? Incest victims leave their bodies and float around elsewhere so the body being assaulted is just flesh and bone, not spirit. Is there a greater sense of abuse than being sliced open and reorganized with few guarantees of success? Of course people in surgery leave their bodies and hang around near the ceiling. Of *course*.

Some people will say that to improve my relationship with John I could simply have answered his question. But that's kicking a man when he's down. And he might have been able to talk about his feelings then too. That would have been too much. Just the hair sticking up and the new wrinkles around the eyes were already more than I could bear.

I didn't say anything for a while. My mind was frozen. My heart was frozen, except for the pity. The pity, and the part that had suddenly awakened to its power. Its ability to crack a cold man.

He waited. I cleared my throat, which seemed to release him, and he sat. Maybe he thought I was preparing to speak.

Pity is disgusting, above all when mistaken for love. When I put my hand on his thigh and slid it toward him with uncharacteristic firmness, most of me screamed in revolt and flew to the other end of the room. Sirens blared in my head until I was deaf. The room telescoped. The couple on the couch shrank. John was left alone on his back, staring unblinking and breathless, completely powerless, into the eyes of a reptile.

I don't want to think about this anymore.

But it's a useful skill, being able to leave your body when you need to.

On Big
Decisions

Pandora likes to sit directly under the lamp on the kitchen table that I turn on when I read the paper. She sits up straight and tall as an Egyptian sculpture, front feet daintily aligned. After a while she falls asleep and her tiny detailed mouth drops open a little. She emits a string of miniature crystal beads. Even when she drools it's dainty.

There wasn't a day in Europe and New York when I didn't wish I had a pet, but how would it have been for the poor thing with me off on trips and visiting lovers? And I don't think any of my beaux felt particularly kindly toward animals. More than one of them got annoyed by how easily animals distracted me when we were out together. Once, with Ted, I went mushy over a tottering old dog, and Ted said, "Lillian, its teeth are *disgusting*."

"Won't ours be one day?" I snapped in response, and immediately regretted it, not so much because of the shift from disgust to dismay on Ted's face but more because of the image from *Death in Venice* I had conjured in my own mind. Horrible book. And my bottom teeth were a little wonky already, so it was best not to draw attention to them. But meeting animals is always such a nice moment for me, even if I don't get to pet the dog at the café or the cat on the arm of the sofa. Just looking at them I feel good, and I coo, and the man talking to me looks irritated.

Someone tried to cure me of this once. It was when I was with Alec, a few years after John. We were away on one of our eating and riding weekends. It must have been 1965, in Herefordshire, at a bed-and-breakfast attached to a farm. We rode at a different stable, but this farm had ponies, and we were walking from stable door to stable door, meeting them. In the corner box there was a beautiful long-legged hunting dog lying in the straw with her puppies. Alec un-latched the lower door as if he owned the place and let us in, which of course made the new mother very anxious, and while I really wanted to stay and touch her I thought we should leave her alone, but when I turned around to pull Alec back outside the farmer was coming in. As well fed a man as Alec, but with ruddier skin. Tweed cap, army-green Wellington boots, dark green quilted jacket over more tweed, not a kind bone in his body. "That's not the whole lot," he nearly bellowed as he took possession of the small space. "There was a runt as well. Knocked him on the head." He reached up to the top ledge of the dusty window and took down the tiny dead bundle. Immediately the bitch was on her feet, scattering her living brood, sniffing and whining and pleading, but the farmer just put the corpse back up on the ledge and smiled at its wretched mother. I could see him looking at a wife that way, calling her The Little Woman to his friends. Alec looked on. I could see a resemblance in the two men that made my heart contract. They thought of themselves as realists, but they were merely brutal.

Some women are amazing. They simply do whatever occurs to them. There was a night in London, years and years ago. A dinner party at Victor and Nancy Ball's, people from the magazine. They had found a cat in the garbage of an alley a few months before. It still felt it had to fight to survive, and they let it. I learned after the first time not to wear stockings I cared about if I was invited over. That night, while we were having drinks and I was running an ice cube up and down the angry scratches on my ankles, Nancy set half a dozen gorgeous dishes of food out on the sideboard. I was talking to a Russian woman named Lyena, a tiny bottle blond in a tight royal blue dress. Her eyes were a very light brown, I recall, with flecks of yellow. I remember because I thought they didn't go with the dress at all, which was a shame. It was distracting. Then of course the cat jumped up on the sideboard. Victor picked it up and put it in the hall, but it was back in seconds. He put it farther down the hall, and this time I think he even said "No" to it. Back it came, determined to be quick this time. We all looked at Victor, of course, the other couple and Lyena and I, and he shrugged. "Must be a Communist," he said, and I felt Lyena bristle and get up from the sofa. She marched over to the sideboard and delivered a speech to the cat in Russian, pointing right at its nose, then she picked it up by the scruff of its neck and threw it into the hallway so that it skidded a few feet on its claws before flashing away into a bedroom.

"Communists wait," she said, "like cows," and sat again, looking around for the drink she had put down.

I wait. There are things I need to throw down my hallway and all the way out the door, but I can't. There have been people too. One, above all. Laszlo. He came along in London and exploded my relationship with John, and that was fine, but continuing the affair was not. John had been cold, and Laszlo was so hot. I don't know what type of woman can handle that much heat, but I'm pretty sure they're not produced in Missouri. Men like that can't listen. They're always planning. Some of them know to say "Oh yes?" from time to time when you're talking, but usually they think all you want to hear about is how they feel in your presence. It's funny. Neither cold men nor hot men will tell you much about how they feel about the wider world.

Laszlo called one evening and I told him with my heart beating in my throat that I really appreciated his attention but that I was very busy and couldn't offer him what he desired. "I'll take anything," he said. "Crumbs from the table, the wine that drips down the side of the glass."

"Crumbs?" I asked.

"Crumbs from you are like the *plat principal* of someone else," he said.

"How do you know?" I asked. It was a ridiculous conversation.

"Please try," he pleaded.

I thought for a bit. "Okay," I said, "I'll see you on Saturdays."

There was silence on the other end of the line and my momentary surge of confidence and power gave way to concern that I had offended him. But then he said, "Darling. You won't regret it."

I did, though. For a few weeks I only saw him on Saturdays, but he called constantly in between, and when I saw him he was so frantic with desire I cringed. When a man I'd flirted with in Paris came over to London for work, I accepted his invitation for a weekend away. I came back so refreshed. He'd allowed me to talk, and had actually responded to what I said. But practically everyone I knew in London told me Laszlo had called them to find out where I was.

The very next Monday evening I was walking near Sloane Square to pick up some shoes and Laszlo came out of a shirtmaker's a little farther down the block. My heart sank but I smiled. He didn't, of course. He just stood and stared and even from a distance I could see how the hurt in his eyes made them turn black. I said, "Hi, Laszlo," as I got nearer, but his mouth didn't move and now I could see the muscles bunching along his jaw. He clearly wasn't going to speak, so I started to move over a bit to walk by him, and to tell the truth I was a little worried I might get burned by the heat coming off him. He was practically shimmering. But as I changed course he shot out an arm and grabbed me by the hair, and I gasped as he pulled me right up close to him. There were plenty of people on the sidewalk, joining friends for dinner after work or dealing with a few errands, like me. But they walked on around us, and I could hear the paper of their bags bumping against their legs as they passed by, and Laszlo continued to hold a big hunk of my hair in his long, desperate fingers. He didn't say anything at all. His mouth was right by my ear, and I listened and listened but I guess his fingers said everything.

God. The things we put ourselves through.

Eventually he let go. The gesture was dismissive. I was glad for that, since I knew he had a better chance of preserving his manliness that way. But even so, dizzying waves of humiliation accompanied my first footsteps along the sidewalk away from him. Actually, they accompanied my footsteps for the next few days.

Every once in a while, as I've grown stronger, I've replayed that scene, and I've made myself imagine reaching up with my own long fingers to calmly disentangle his and replace his hand by his side and walk away. Sometimes I simultaneously disentangle his fingers from my hair and break his pinkie. In another version I stay still until he lets go, and when he thinks I'm going to walk away I take him by the shoulders, the first shoulders that ever loomed over me, and push him backward through the shirtmaker's display window. The crash is dazzling, and then I see Laszlo lying in the shards. He's not bloody—I couldn't handle that—but he's stunned, with an expensive sleeve flopped across his head. *Then* I walk away. I bet that's happened in somebody's life. There's a woman out there who could do that. I never will, though.

When I had Pandora's front claws removed because she was destroying the furniture, I took courage from the memory of Lyena. I'd never have the grit to throw my kitty down a hallway, but I mustered enough to have her claws removed and rule out the need ever to have that battle. It took me forever to decide on that expensive upholstery fabric. At least two years. You can only make a big decision like that so many times.

On the
Danger of
Water

When you wash your hands, you get to thinking. Maybe you take off your ring and put it on the corner of the sink in the public toilet you've just used, right where you can see it, with every intention to put it back on once your hands are dry, like you do at home. But human beings are weaker than water. You turn it on and your thoughts start flowing. You lather up and they slide even farther away, and when you walk from the sink to the hand towels you are anywhere but in that public toilet, and you walk out.

When you go back, mouth dry, tongue thick, you're willing so hard for the ring still to be there that when it's not you can practically see those cartoon lines that indicate the absence of something. It is a cartoon sometimes, my life. I lose everything, at least for a little while.

When I lost the ring that Poppa bought me I thought I'd kill myself. That ring was me. Poppa put it on my hand when I turned thirty-five and admired it, chuckling happily to himself, as he often did. It was summer, and I'd done my fingernails in bright pink, and the opal looked so at home on my hand. The little diamonds surrounding it smiled in the sun coming through the breakfast bay windows.

The night before, after flying in from New York, I barely had time to unpack and bathe before sweet Eunice from two houses down was over for dinner with her coconut pie and Poppa was pouring drinks from crystal decanters. I have those now, as well as the necklaces they wear that identify their contents: scotch, gin, bourbon, vodka. Engraved in silver.

Mother didn't frighten Eunice. Maybe Eunice saw the good in Mother. She was the only woman I never heard Mother say a word against, so when Eunice was there, I caught a glimmer of the good in Mother too.

I'd brought Mother cigarettes from duty-free, as usual, and cologne for Poppa. He'd put it on, I was sure. Mother and I smoked together, and Eunice asked questions about Paris, and we were all too polite to remind her that I'd moved to London. When she got up to leave I bent down and hugged her and felt none of what I did hugging Mother. No oversized pearls at my collarbone, no big buttons catching my belt, no hipbones in my thigh. Eunice was as warm and soft as a muffin.

Poppa was clearing up the bar, collecting squeezed slices of lemon and lime, emptying the footed silver ice bucket, and Mother announced she was going up. I thought I'd climb the stairs with her; I recalled she had a bit of trouble with them at the end of the day. We went up at her pace. Halfway to the landing I said, "Thirty-five tomorrow. Can you believe it?"

Mother snorted. "Thirty-five," she said. "Unmarried." I heard our shoes making a rhythmic *shush, shush, shush* on the pale blue carpet. On the landing, we walked a few steps, then she needed to go left to their room, and mine was straight ahead. I turned to kiss her good night and she fixed me with an angry look.

"Even if you were divorced, at least you would have *done* it," she said.

It was the next morning that Poppa gave me the ring and chuckled to himself. Mother was at the counter in a navy dress and red lipstick making Sanka. By the time she sat down with us the moment was over. I put the ringed hand under the table, and Poppa took it in his.

On Looking
the Part

D id Mother get married for the sake of getting married? I don't want to think so. I want her to have fallen madly in love with Poppa. I wanted to marry. It pains me that she imagined I was being insubordinate rather than unlucky.

I like to think I don't regret anything. *Rien de rien*, as the song goes. But if I think about Alec too long, I feel regret like a cloud of lead.

Alec was very tall, and broad, and had been bred to pass judgment. Even I was aware we looked very smart together. The first time he picked me up for dinner he looked me over and nodded once in approval, to himself it seemed, checking off some sort of box in his head. It irritated me but I tingled. In the restaurant he ordered for us both, which was also irritating, but if I've learned anything from life with other men, it is to keep my distance from male pride. It's an electric fence.

Alec had ideas for my wardrobe, just like Willis. It's funny how some men don't even notice clothes, like John, and others need them. Alec helped me buy riding things.

Really good jodhpurs and a short jacket flecked with brown and black, one color to go with my eyes and one with my hair. I would have liked to be able to choose the clothes myself, but I'd only ever ridden in jeans. Afterward I did feel closer to Alec, something he appeared to intuit. He nodded to himself on the way from the shops to the car and said, "Tonight we go to bed." I pretended not to notice.

Pretending not to notice is the key to so much, I believe.

When I was seventeen years old my mother had my portrait painted. It was my coming-out painting. I'm seated with my hands in my lap with my knees pointing left and my head turned toward the viewer. The only thing that's really coming out is my neck. I've got a pearl choker on. The dress is white and sleeveless, fitted to the waist and with a full skirt. In reality, the dress had a detail of extremely sheer organza, sort of like a collar, from shoulder to shoulder. The artist decided not to paint it. Maybe it was too difficult. But I think not. If he could capture the way I sat up straight and tall because I was told to and not because I felt strong and upright, he could certainly paint a hint of organza. But the artist decided not to cover me up. Not to make me modest. It was a portrait of a girl who looked as if she had been surrounded by silver-backed hairbrushes all her life. If you didn't know me, you might even see the look as haughty.

Going to bed with Alec was my first experience of silver-backed hairbrushes, and of monogrammed sheets, and I brought Mother's Missouri demons into bed with us. I knew I was an impostor, as she would have. After seven years in Europe, after Le Cordon Bleu and John, I knew how to order food, but Alec ordered for me. I knew that eventually he'd recognize that he did so not out of chivalry but because he was ordering what he wanted me to want.

One of the things he seemed to love about me was that I drove that little old Jag around the city. I'd brought it over from Paris on the ferry when I moved. "Here's my speed queen," he'd say loudly to his friends when I'd show up at a restaurant desperate to get my hair in place before reaching the table. Everyone would look. But I only drove that car because Willis gave it to me. That car said more about Willis than it did about me.

On the morning I began to wonder if I was pregnant, I was sitting in the tea shop up the road from my apartment. It was a Sunday morning. I had the *Times*—weighty and full of the promise of knowledge and wonder and regret—on the chair next to me. The waitress brought me my scrambled egg, fried tomato and mushrooms, two pieces of toast, and butter and jam in tiny brown ceramic bowls. There was hardly any jam at all. I should have asked her for more right then, but I let her go, and I ate my eggs, pushing them onto my fork with a piece of toast very thinly covered with raspberry preserves. When I called the waitress over to show her my empty jam bowl and ask for more, my tea was getting cold, but I didn't ask for another pot. She came back with the little jam bowl overflowing. Now I had much too much. Suddenly it was too difficult. Tears stung my eyes but I smiled and thanked her.

If there's anything I can't stand it's jam an inch thick, the way George Junior spreads it. I put some of the jam on my second and last piece of toast and ate it. Raspberry jam is so delicious, especially when its tang is set off by good fresh butter. I had some of both left. Before I knew it I had taken the teaspoon from my saucer, had used it to get the remainder of the butter and the large dollop of jam out of their bowls, and had put all of it into my mouth. It was heaven. It made me want to cry again. I felt hot and prickly. I felt like I had a need no amount of jam and butter could ever satisfy. I went through the motions of reading the paper.

The following evening I left the office without my

handbag. Two days later I walked out of a tea shop without paying. When I was with Alec, I just let him take care of all our arrangements as usual, and listened more than I talked, which wasn't too strange. On the next weekend I left my handbag in a gallery. Things kept falling off me, even more than usual.

My body talked to my brain and I understood what was happening. I admitted to myself that I was pregnant as I walked through Regent's Park to meet a visiting friend from Paris at her hotel. I can only approximate the way this felt by describing a dove whose foot is tied to a stone by an elastic thread. The beautiful dove began to fly inside me; I felt its good soft breast against my heart, lifting my chest, lightening my ribs. The cold stone began to sink. The thread stretched and reached its full extension. Joy battled dread. I could be a mother. Alec wasn't kind enough to be the father. He'd be dismissive. He would never massage our child's feet. He'd mock my instincts. He'd make fun of my strengths as well as my weaknesses. And no matter what he decided on, for my dinner or my wardrobe, I'd still be an impostor.

I had to cut the dove free, leaving only the stone, which couldn't be dislodged. By the time I reached the hotel I knew I'd terminate.

I hate that something so physically beautiful as a pregnancy can turn out to be so emotionally ugly. On top of it all, *abortion* is such a disgusting word. It sounds exactly like the flushing of a toilet. Is there any word, even *flush*, that sounds more so? Disgusted, alone, resolved, I stepped out of the park to cross the road and have tea in an overstuffed silk chair across from my smiling friend.

How effectively an abortion ends a relationship. If it had been love, there would have been no abortion. Even if it meant a baby soon after the wedding. If the wedding is dazzling enough, loving enough, elegant enough, if everyone's smiling and beautiful, even if it rains, and no corners are cut, the guests will forgive you anything.

Alec was sitting in his armchair reading his *Financial Times* when I told him. It was a Sunday morning, a week after my decision. The sun was still quite low, knifing through the window to point out the bowl of roses on the table by Alec's elbow. Always a bowl of roses. I bet putting roses in bowls was first done by peasants. Peasants didn't own vases. When they couldn't jam them in a jug because it was full of milk or ale, they'd use bowls. I bet. But a bowl of roses became classy. I put bowls of flowers in my apartment a lot too, but never roses, not after that day. Peonies, usually.

"I thought you might be," Alec said, turning a page. "What are you going to do?"

I had imagined he might ask what *we* were going to do, or what I would *like* to do. Then I would be able to say I'd made a decision, and feel strong but also appreciative. The fact of that "you," the fact that he already insisted the decision was mine alone, took my breath away. He turned another page.

"I'll set you up somewhere," he said. Maybe he thought this was what my silence was intended to drag out of him.

"Oh, Alec," I said, standing up, finally crying, finally being honest with him. "You have such a horrible personality."

On the
Way to Go

That night I had dinner with my friend Nigel. Where Alec was an oak, Nigel was a weed. His eyes were limpid, his metaphors dripping with feeling. His hands were long and gentle. I could relax with Nigel.

"So he's an ox," he said over the cod. "But I knew that already, at the beginning."

"And you didn't say anything, you dog."

"Men like me don't get in the way of men like him. Words don't work."

"What works?"

"Oxen need to be penned. Otherwise they run amok. Trample villages."

"Well," I said, "this one's populated mine."

"Yes," he said, and he touched my arm with those long gentle fingers.

"Come with me," I blurted.

"Of course," he said, completely matter-of-factly, forking up some boiled potato.

Waking up from the anesthetic was one of my life's worst moments. I was so, so cold, but my forearm was warm because of Nigel's hand on it. He was sitting by the bed, reading a book. I watched him for a while, waiting for better control of my groggy eyes before letting him know I was conscious.

Gay men love me. There have been times when I'm sure one wished he *were* me. Something about my neck and my dramatic hair. But also because I've had to suspend judgment for so long. The culture shock of Europe knocked the ability to judge other people's behavior right out of me. Nobody came from where I came from or felt what I felt, so I adapted. Gay men loved how unconventionally I lived, I think. But I wanted to get married and have children. That had been the plan. Lovers and wine, cigarettes and skinny black clothes—those were the detritus on the rings circling the planet of my dreams. I was in orbit and I couldn't find my way across the void.

I still am. I still can't. Gay men take the edge off, though. They notice when I change my hairstyle, and help me move furniture, give me tours of their window boxes and invite me for Thanksgiving when there's no family in town. They save me from the cold.

When I die, if I can't have six former lovers as my pall-bearers, I want six strapping gay men instead. Some will be stoically clenching their teeth and making their jaw muscles dance; some will be singing lustily with tears streaming down their cheeks.

On Not
Loving
the Help

I need a haircut. I had my hair washed and styled before Michael arrived, but I'm crazy if I think that will keep it under control. I'm lucky that I can brush it off my face and it will stay there, though. It doesn't flop around now that it's white, and stiffer. But it's not neat. Everyone else in the family's was. All our hair went prematurely gray, and mine went white even before George Junior's. But his got really thin, so I didn't complain. Poppa's was white on his pink scalp. Mother had that blue rinse that looks pale lavender. She continued to wear her bold red dresses as if her hair were white, which I saw as a mistake.

One summer George Junior and I coordinated a visit back to Columbia so that we could see each other. It must have been sometime in the late seventies, since Zoë was about ten, which would make me forty-two. I wanted to see her. George Junior had also got Mother to invite Mary over so we could see her again. Or maybe that was for Zoë's sake. I had just returned to New York from a board meeting in Munich. I'd been up all night drafting the minutes before flying down, so after a family lunch—some sort of

Wonder Bread casserole; it was eternally 1955 in Mother's kitchen—I went upstairs to lie down, as my parents did. I knew Mary was due in the early afternoon. I thought I'd just close my eyes for fifteen minutes or so. I never do this. Over an hour later I woke up snoring. Not the way Poppa snored. He was like an outboard motor with gallons and gallons of gas to run on. I snore in starts, like a startled pig.

I didn't know where I was at first, or what the time could possibly be. When I began to recognize my old room, the silly pale blue curtains that never fully opened, I fleetingly wondered when Mary would be coming to get me for breakfast. I lifted my head and saw my adult body. I saw my black blouse and remembered putting it on for the flight, remembered Ted unbuttoning it in Germany a few days before, remembered not having much time to pack, remembered putting in a gift for Zoë, remembered Zoë, remembered Mary. My heart skipped a beat. I swung my legs off the bed and walked through several yards of mental fog to the bathroom.

The facecloth was dusty. It had obviously been hanging a long time on the towel rack. That was how Mother felt a bathroom should look, whether or not there were visitors. It's true: A bathroom without towels on the racks looks abandoned. Towels and facecloths are good. But this facecloth clearly hadn't been put out expressly for me. I used a corner of it to freshen my face. I combed my hair. I went down the light blue stairs to see if Mary had arrived.

I heard her before I reached the bottom of the stairs. She was speaking slowly, and her voice was a little rough, but it was Mary. "Yeah, Russell's doin' fine, I thank yeh," she was saying, and I pictured coming around the corner and throwing my arms around her. When I reached the bottom of the stairs and looked into the living room on my left, I saw that I couldn't fulfill this fantasy. Mary was sitting on the big footstool of the armchair by the grand piano, with the front windows behind her and a side table moved next to her for her coffee cup. George Junior was crouched on one knee in front of her, looking up into her face with an expression I couldn't identify as closer to awe or closer to begging for forgiveness. Mary wasn't looking at him, but had her face tipped up a little proudly. Mother had told us she was almost blind, so she was just listening, not looking. She wasn't offering much. We had invited her and she had come. She was answering George Junior's questions, that was all. Judy and Zoë were watching from over by the fireplace. "Russ's got three grandkiddies now," she was saying.

"So that means you have how many great-grandchildren?" asked George Junior.

"I have eleven," she said.

"Wow!" I said from the stairs. I couldn't help it. Everyone turned my way, except Mary. She just waited. I wanted her to say, "Come here, missy," but she didn't. George Junior got to his feet, kind of reluctantly I thought, giving me the space to hurry over and bend down and kiss her. She smelled of talcum powder and hair oil and warm polyester. Her hairline scratched my face and I realized she was wearing a wig. I wondered if her hair was white too, underneath. If she could have seen me clearly, would she have preferred a black wig over my white hair? I sat at her feet.

"You sure love the floor, you two." We laughed. "I don't remember you ever sitting on the floor as children. You was always sitting up straight and proud as can be at that fancy old dining table."

George Junior said, "Mother and Dad are upstairs asleep now, aren't they, Mary? So we can do what we want."

Mary wheezed a bit at this, in her way. She'd never look at you when she laughed, not in the eye. That would have been a shared moment I suppose. She stayed above us, God bless her. And now her eyes were milky and upturned.

"How much can you see, Mary?" I asked.

"I can see Heaven, child," she said regally.

"Wow," said Zoë. Mary nodded as if this were the correct response.

"One thing I'm gonna do when I get there? I'm gonna throw a ball for old Sparky up there, throw it far, toward the Pearly Gates, and watch Sparky run too fast and slow down too late and crash into them gates in his joy."

"Do you have a dog now, Mary?" George Junior asked, laughing.

"No, sir," she said. "Dogs are a terrible nuisance. Nasty too."

"But Sparky was a dog," protested Zoë.

"That Sparky was no dog," Mary replied to the air. "That there was a clown in a dog suit. Crying shame, that was. Crying shame."

I used to come home from middle school, when George Junior was already gone, and I'd throw the ball down the hall next to the kitchen. Mother was often out, and Mary'd be in the kitchen saying "Ouchie!" every time Sparky hit the wall. In his joy Sparky used to run after the paperboy on his bicycle. The paperboy panicked each time, and one day when Sparky got too close he kicked him as hard as he could. Sparky died a few days later. One day he seemed fine, still joyful. Then he convulsed and died.

Once Sparky was gone, I'd come home and sit in the kitchen talking to Mary, or if Mother was there I'd talk to Mother and send my thoughts to Mary, who'd keep chopping quietly and didn't seem to care one way or another. Then one day, at the beginning of high school, there was no one chopping in the kitchen.

"Where's Mary?"

"We don't need her anymore, honey, so she's working for the Tremains."

"I need her!"

Mother turned from the sink. She was washing perfect tomatoes. Her tomatoes always grew perfectly. "What do *you* need her for?"

That was hard to answer.

Mother turned back to the sink. "You see? You're a young woman. Chop your mother some onions."

I needed Mary's hugs. Mother would put her arms around me at her cocktail parties and then slap me on the hip so that everyone could hear. It made my eyes sting. I'd always say, "*Ow*, Mother," and she'd say, "Aw, *honey*, it's just a love pat." I wasn't concerned whether Mary loved me or not. It was enough that she didn't criticize my looks or my friends. What concerned me was that I loved her. I could tell her what I wanted to tell her, and it would stay with her, just as I told it, and not become something else. Mary kept secrets. Or maybe she just forgot what I said, but it felt like she kept secrets, which was good enough. But I was sure, sitting there on the floor in front of her under my white hair, that she didn't think about seeing me in Heaven. So I asked.

"Think I'll get to Heaven, Mary?"

"No, child," she said. "You're too full of mischief."

"Ha!" I said, delighted. "How do you know?"

"Who knows but me?"

We were all smiling, and didn't talk for a while. Zoë fidgeted.

"More coffee, Mary?" asked Judy, who understood that neither George Junior nor I would initiate a parting. Mary clearly hadn't touched the cup on the side table.

"No, I thank yeh. There's Russell anyway."

The doorbell rang. Only she had heard his footsteps on the walk.

George Junior stepped forward and offered his hand to help her up but she didn't see it. "Lots of things to do before Heaven," he said, putting his hand under hers to make the offer clear.

"Couple three," she agreed.

Zoë giggled at the expression, and tried it out. "Couple three."

"At least," said Mary, heaving to her swollen feet.

Judy and Zoë stayed where they were while Mary accepted kisses from George Junior and me. Russell, such a big man now, leaned forward and helped his mother down the stairs and along the path to the car. George Junior and I stood side by side, white-haired, almost the same height, and watched them go. We turned toward each other to return to the living room and he put an arm around me, so of course I started to cry. I should never have been left alone with Mary as a child. She knew me, and I'd never see her again. *Better to have loved and lost than never to have loved at all* is just so much rubbish sometimes.

On White

Why did I buy these paper napkins? Tartan? Things so often look better in the shop than in your home, where there are so many other things to compete with. I wish everything in my apartment were white, actually, except maybe the geraniums on the windowsills and the fruit on the dining table. A white porcelain soup tureen, even if you never use it, even if it sits for decades on the sideboard, can make you feel clean and calm. Imagine opening it to reveal red pepper soup. Red berry tea in delicate white cups on a glass table touched with sunlight. An ostrich egg. I used to have one, don't know where it is now, but I could put my hand on its excellent cool shape and feel a funny connection.

I read somewhere that the reason Japanese advertising is often so simple and peaceful, always giving the impression of a light breeze blowing through, is that such an atmosphere is just a dream in that country, almost impossible to achieve when living cheek by jowl. I leaf through my magazines—*Architectural Digest, House & Garden, Vanity Fair*—and I pull out the pages of my dreams. White curtains blowing out over the back of a white couch. White shelves supporting a few white objects—porcelain, shell, faded wood, rice paper.

Colors keep crowding me, but it's my fault. I'd have everything white if I were organized.

Even love hasn't had the power to clear my clutter.

There was an awful day after I moved to the New York bureau when I had to reconstruct the board meeting minutes and I couldn't find my notes. I was scared and ashamed and Ted said to me, "Do you know why the ropes are always coiled in the same way in the same place on yachts, Lillian?" Of course I didn't. I was a deer in headlights. I'd been on yachts, but I hadn't thought about the ropes. "It's so that when things get dicey and everyone needs to keep the boat safe and sailing, there's no question as to where things are and what's been done with them. You can put your hand on anything you need because it's always where it should be in the way it should be there." He spread his big hands, palms up, to indicate the mountain of papers and magazines on my desk, and left.

A few months before, Ted and I had worked late and made love on the floor of his office until even later. I don't know what Ted needed to work on that night, but I was as usual trying to catch up. The sun went down and I finished typing, separated the copies from the carbon paper, left mine on my desk and took Ted's into his office, thinking simultaneously about how I'd need to wash my hands well in order not to get blue on my dress and about how handsome Ted was with his sleeves rolled up, reading in the light of his desk lamp, chewing his lip. A big man chewing his lip is an attractive, vulnerable thing. A small man chewing his lip is a rodent.

I could have stayed opposite him and handed him the papers across his desk, but something kept me walking around to stand on his left. Maybe I manufactured something to point out to him. His face was a few inches from my arm. He turned his head slowly and rested his lips on my blouse, and I could feel the warmth seeping through the fabric and into my skin, and neither of us moved. Sometimes the grandest moments are the quietest. Then he dropped his left hand and pressed the backs of his fingers against my calf, and the colors crowded in.

When he told me I needed to be shipshape three months later, I wanted to be shipshape. I came in on the weekend in slacks and rolled-up sleeves and cut the mountain down to size. By Sunday afternoon I was standing by the filthy window, chewing on a heel of bread, feeling like a normal person.

Sunday night I washed and styled my hair, cleaned up my cuticles and painted my nails. Monday morning I put on a gray skirt and a long red cashmere sweater. It was early December. Sitting in my office, I tapped my nails on the clean top of my desk and allowed one piece of paper at a time onto my blotter. Of course it didn't last. Systems don't stick with me. I forget I even *have* systems sometimes. But that was a lovely moment in a strange, strange day.

At lunchtime Ted came in and said, "You're coming with me." It sounded professional, maybe something had gone wrong in Munich again, but he took me into the elevator, which could only mean we were leaving the building.

"Everything okay?" I ventured.

"Yep," he said, then he cleared his throat, the doors opened and we walked briskly out of the building, straight to the corner and left on Forty-ninth Street. A block and a half down he turned to look behind us, took my hand and pulled me through a dark door past photos I had no time to take in. We ducked through deep red velvet curtains and were in a small cinema. The movie had already started and the tiny space was full of the lip-smacking noises of a man sucking on a hugely endowed woman's nipples. Ted exhaled audibly, squeezing my hand. I looked at him and he looked down at me. "Safe," he whispered, and had me follow him

into a pair of seats. I looked at the screen, and I looked at
Ted looking at the screen. After a bit he leaned toward me,
not taking his eyes off the ecstatic couple. "Okay?" he asked.
I wasn't sure, but he looked so thrilled. So boyish, and also
so powerfully male.

Mother was a constant stream of what you couldn't do,
what wasn't done. I could only imagine Ted's wife was similar in her way. She kept very busy volunteering and orga-
nizing charity galas and performing in amateur theatricals.
I think she also wrote some of them. Her hair was still
Jackie Kennedy long after Jackie was Onassis. She made
picnics for the family to eat in Central Park on weekends.
So I put my hand on his crotch.

People say that some things are meant to be. The question that doesn't get answered, or even asked, is *what* these
things are meant to be. Then there are more questions. I
can say I was meant to be with Ted. But then, what does
with mean? Or even *be*? He was completely under my skin.
He still is. His breath crawls beneath the first layer. His
ghost is the air under that. How much more with can you
get? How much more be?

I was never allowed to make visible marks on him. We
washed my blue carbon-paper fingerprints off him after
that first time. But I once had a dream in which I was alone

in a peaceful white room. There wasn't any furniture, just curved white walls in a perfect circle around me. No windows to complicate the sight, just light streaming down from high above. I turned around and around, studying the room. Then I stopped, reached into my pocket and pulled out a ring. It was a beautiful ring of platinum and precious stones, not something I recognized when I woke up but in the dream it was absolutely mine. I went over to the perfectly white wall, and started using the ring to draw on it, just like a caveman: "I was here. Something happened. I want you to know."

On One-Night Stands

I always tell Judy when I take someone to bed. I don't know why. She's always disapproving, and her eyes go a little wild. She lets me tell her, though. She's never said she doesn't want to know. And she keeps sending people to stay with me for the few nights they're in town for meetings or a reunion.

It's usually the wine. Red, above all. I love to drink it, and if they love to drink it too, then when we head for the bedroom it's really like all we've done is dive in. The sheets are waves of wine moving over us as we swim in the glass.

Judy even sent me a lord once. And then she was aghast when he proved temptable. Either she's been married too long, or not long enough. To tell the truth, though, Alfred kept a polite distance for so long that I thought I'd be sleeping alone that night. He spent a lot of time staring bemusedly into his glass. I was at the head of the table and he was sitting to my left, so I had a view of his profile for most of dinner. The candles made the wine look as velvet as usual, and he seemed to enjoy looking at it more than drinking it. Eventually I got tired of studying his lips and looked at his ear. I've studied my share of aristocrats, and had expected the long lobes that tend to accompany the narrow nose and tall forehead of the aging gentry. His were small, though; they were the first I'd ever seen that truly reminded me of shells. Even if I hadn't been drinking, I think they would have touched my heart. They were a child's ears. We had been talking about Budapest—he'd just been—but his silence had lulled me into imagining that touching him would have no effect. It was peaceful. I reached out to feel the perfect inside of his ear, forgetting it was attached to a man. I was startled when he leaned into my hand—

This is how I told the story to Judy. I think I went on about his ear for a really long time, actually. The truth is, I studied his ear after he fell asleep. I always do this. I study the sleeping profile and imagine that I'm seeing it for the four thousandth time. So the truth is I didn't touch his ear at the dinner table. I eventually said, "You'd be welcome in my room tonight, Alfred." He continued staring into his glass. I slipped my left foot out of my shoe and put it on his thigh. If he gave my foot firmly back to me, I'd say, *Never mind, I completely understand,* but he wrapped his hand around it and squeezed. He squeezed so hard that it hurt, but it didn't feel like *You whore*, it felt like *Yes*, so I blew out the candle closest to me and he blew out the other and I had him.

"Oh, Lillian, not *Alfred*," Judy said. I made up the ear story on the spot, told her how maternal it made me feel, how curious, and how I'd had to change gears entirely when he responded to my touch. I doubt she believed me but she was too polite to press it. We were at their house when I told her all this. George Junior was playing the piano in the living room. I was chopping vegetables for gazpacho. She was slicing crusty bread in her determined way.

"Isn't it awkward in the morning?" she asked after a time, then sliced more quietly to hear my answer.

"Never has been," I said, transferring vegetables from cutting board to blender. "Not when we both know it's not going to happen again. Alfred was up and dressed, reading the paper when I got up. I've learned not to talk too much in the mornings, to let them come to me. I go about in my nightie for a bit, drinking my coffee, and they join me if they feel like it and don't if they don't. Then I dress. Saying goodbye clothed has a nice finality to it." I switched on the blender and the beautiful bright tomatoes, peppers, cucumbers and onions leaped and danced and dissolved. I turned it off and the quiet was fragrant. "If Ted leaves me in the morning I like still to be in my nightie. The goodbye embrace is so intimate that way. But with others, *les passants*, I'm dressed, totally pulled together. New day. Page turned. Unless . . . No."

Judy brought me three bowls. "Unless what?"

"Nothing."

Unless they've already left when I wake up.

When I went into the office on the day after Ted and I made love for the first time, I wondered if he'd behave coldly, or come out and tell me it had been a mistake that couldn't be repeated. I prepared myself for business as usual, and business only. If I'd felt more confident, I would have gone in to the office early, to be alone with him before the workday started, to get up close and smell him again. I was awake before the alarm, but I made myself wait. I didn't want him to feel awkward being alone with me. I changed my nail color and I looked again at the impossible parts of Sunday's crossword. I thought through a dozen outfits, and decided black would be best. A-line skirt, long-sleeved top, stockings, heavy silver earrings. Serious.

I said good morning to people as I walked through the newsroom to my office outside Ted's, but not overbrightly. I tried to look like I was thinking about a meeting. He wasn't at his desk when I got there and I just went to work, pretending there was saliva in my mouth when it was bone dry. I had something to type that required three pieces of typing paper and two pieces of carbon paper. It took forever to get the pages lined up and another eternity to get them behaving themselves on the cylinder. I swore at the thing, and he arrived in the doorway just in time to hear it.

"Does your mother know you use words like that?" he asked as he moved toward the door to his office, smiling. I picked up a pen and my notebook, as usual in the morning, and followed him.

"My mother doesn't know much about me at all," I said.

He went behind his desk and sat down facing me. "Oh? You don't tell her much?"

"Not anymore."

We were both smiling. Smiling to beat the band. I thought we weren't going to be able to stop, and then a look I couldn't interpret traveled across his face. It looked a bit like sadness, but maybe it was shyness. He glanced away from me and inhaled, and when he finally looked back he was smiling again, but warmly this time.

"Would you like some more things not to tell your mother about?" he said, and a nipple-hardening rash of joy scorched my torso.

Whenever I leave after telling Judy about my sex life, I know she tells George Junior my stories. I worry a little about that. But if I've learned anything, it's this: The world has never loved a spinster, and never will. The more people she tells, the merrier.

On Memory's Mismatched Moments

J udy sent me Michael, actually, nearly three years ago. They'd known each other in college, and he'd looked her up when he was on his way to New York to do research on UN policy in Ethiopia. He's such a smart man. He stayed for three weeks, and during that time he said one of the loveliest things anyone's ever said to me, and we were robbed at gunpoint.

All my early memories of him are in jagged pieces. I hate that we live really lovely moments as well as moments of true horror with people. Wouldn't it feel so much better if we had only charming experiences with some people, and only hideous experiences with others? Then we'd know what to do.

He came in from Philadelphia. I picked him up at Penn Station and drove him back to my apartment via the sights. He'd been before, many times of course, but was very charming from the outset. I got the feeling he was a bit dazzled. I can tell. He said he'd love to see everything through my eyes. "Sometimes this city seems so chaotic, doesn't it?" he said, "And sometimes it seems so beautifully laid out." As I was to be, later that night. I could just feel it, immediately. He talked slowly, belying his drive. There is no languor in Michael. We agreed, driving past Rockefeller Center, that Judy's voice was like a silver bell, and that George Junior's waters ran deep. At the apartment he was appreciative of the guest room, and unpacked immediately. When I told him I was going to do some shopping, he said he'd like to walk the neighborhood. It was summer, and all the produce looked inviting. Well, it was, in the truest sense; that was the point of all that color and juice and life. I bought strawberries and raspberries and endives and lemons. I bought smoked salmon, and bread, and French cheeses. I bought white wine this time.

He got my whole story out of me at dinner, except for Ted. I talked about Willis. Michael said no one described Paris better than Americans in love. After dinner he asked for the story of every photo on the wall that leads to my room, and spent a long time dissecting a black-and-white portrait of Zoë, age nine, in a high-necked party dress and lip gloss. He went on at length about her sense of self and her sophistication, and I didn't think at all about whether this corresponded with her nature. I luxuriated instead in the music of a man spending time in the head of a girl. My back was tingling because I could feel my open bedroom door behind us, but I didn't let myself interrupt him. When he'd finished, he looked up at my coming-out painting. "And this is you?" he said. I nodded apologetically. "No," he said, putting his hands on my ribs. "*This* is you." He guided me deftly backward into my room. When he sat me on the bed he noticed the bowl of flowers on the bedside table. "I knew you were the kind of person who would have peonies in the bedroom," he said. That was the loveliest thing. Before he knew about the flowers, he'd been inside my head and he'd seen them.

We went to bed together several times during his stay, always on the same wavelength about what it did or didn't mean. Our schedules dovetailed nicely. It was always after we hadn't seen much of each other for a few days, and had lots of stories to tell at dinner. His research went fairly well, and he was optimistic about it.

When his stay was almost over, we went to an art opening. I parked in a dead-end alley not too far from the gallery, deep inside it so the parking police wouldn't notice. The exhibit was irritating. The artist had refused to give any of her paintings a title, so there was no jumping-off point. Even something as simple as "Yellow #7" gives me an idea of where to begin in my thinking. Michael didn't agree at first, because he said he believed in the complete liberty of the viewer to feel what he felt, without being limited by the perspective of the artist. I told him that no title had ever constrained my ability to have my own personal reaction to a painting, I just wanted to know if my perspective and the artist's were similar or different, and if he was going to smile so condescendingly he could take himself to the bar and get me a glass of wine. We had a good time.

Then a man followed us into the alley. I had my hand in my bag, digging for my keys, and he had followed so quietly that when he spoke and I turned I was looking right into the barrel of his gun. I guess they know that this is the most frightening way to do it. They could point it at your chest with equally fatal results, but then you don't have to look into the barrel. The barrel is like an eye. Just like a camera. If someone pointed a TV camera at my breastbone and asked me to answer questions, I wouldn't have too much trouble, but point that same camera in my face and I'm mute. I couldn't talk, even when the robber had thrown Michael's wallet back at him because there was no money in it and was hissing at me to hurry up. I wanted to say something but all I could do was pull things out of my bag that made other bits and pieces drop out into the alley. When he finally had my wallet I looked at his face, and he looked so frustrated that I was sure he would kill me, so I looked at the gun again. Then he tucked it in his pants and ran away.

Those were the days before hooded sweatshirts, so I could describe him pretty clearly to the police, but they didn't find him. During a moment waiting at the police station, Michael said, "I wish I could have protected you." Poor fellow. I think he had felt chivalrous in my bed, but now that image had been challenged. "Maybe you did," I said.

"By default, you mean?"

I patted his hand.

That night I didn't sleep until dawn. A couple of times I thought of climbing in with Michael, but each time I imagined doing so it was Ted I saw in the bed with me. I wanted him back. Suddenly Michael was more like a brother. Having been threatened together made us family, and smashed into shards the images of us at dinner or laughing on the street or in bed.

Why don't I feel the same way about Ted? Why haven't the bad memories smashed the good ones? Why don't the good ones struggle to maintain their status? I don't know. They just don't. With Ted, even my memories of the most painful events are tinged with the sunrise colors of belonging, and the moments of delight are darkened at the corners by the separation that would always follow. So it all matched. And it's why I couldn't leave.

I tried. After a couple of years I was so tense from wondering about the future that I had to get away. I had plans to spend Christmas with George Junior and Judy at their home in Florida, so I told Ted that when I came back to New York in the new year, things would have to be different. I told him I needed a whole relationship. We were standing across from each other with his desk between us. It was winter, so dark came early. I couldn't see anything outside the window behind him, only us, reflected. I saw myself walk into his office and close the door, and I saw both his front and his back when he stood up. He looked like he was going to come around the desk toward me, so I put up a hand to stop him. I walked right up to the desk, stepping a little to the left so that his body blocked my reflection in the window and I was just looking at him. I leaned my thighs against the desk for support. I said my piece, and when he said, "But," I repeated myself. "I need a whole relationship," I said again, and he dropped his head and looked down. When he did, he noticed that his pants had been rucked up over his crotch like a silly sort of empty erection. I was aware of it, of course, and it was helping me.

He looked unkempt, for once. He looked wrong, for once.
But then he noticed it and he shifted his weight and he
smoothed the fabric, and when he looked back up at me he
was perfectly handsome again. I nearly didn't say the last
thing I had come to say, but when he moved I saw myself
reflected in the window and I had trouble looking myself in
the eye. I stepped back from the desk. "This relationship
has to work for both of us, Ted. Not just you." I walked to
the door and opened it, and I didn't look back before closing
it behind me again.

In Florida, I told George Junior and Judy my news, and
they hugged me and patted me, and I often felt Judy looking
at me carefully to gauge my mental state when I came down
to breakfast in the cold mornings. I concentrated on Zoë,
who must have been about three. Her hair was still blond
back then. I needed to be outside. I felt okay outside, and
took her with me. We rambled around the land the house
sat on. It was covered in enormous oak trees feathered with
Spanish moss, and the ground under our feet was soft and
rust-colored. We walked through a mysterious world and we
made up stories. I held her up to touch soft lichen, and
crouched down with her when she wanted to see where a
bug had gone. I whistled at her when she sucked her finger

because I thought it was time she was done with that, and she'd smile and hide her finger behind her back as if it were something she'd stolen, and then we'd keep playing.

But every once in a while, a couple of times a day, I'd wander off out of their lives and back into my own. I'd be drying dishes, or brushing my hair, and I'd forget where I was. The dishes would be my dishes, the mirror would be my mirror, and I'd fall back into the usual imaginings, the normal daily fare of my mind. When would I be alone with Ted again? When was it he said he'd try to call?

If he'd called when I was holding Zoë, or looking at old photos with George Junior, I might have had a chance, but I was polishing my black pumps for Christmas dinner. There just hadn't been time before I left. I was remembering an evening when we'd been at a cocktail party on a roof, and we'd eased away from the rest of the crowd for a bit, finding some peace and quiet on the far side of the access door. I was feeling a little tipsy, a little reckless, and I stepped up onto the wide low wall around the edge of the roof, using Ted's shoulder for support. "Don't," he said, and I turned my back to him in mischief, looking out at the beautiful cityscape. It was when he put his hands on my hips that I looked down and rocked with a lurch of vertigo. I concentrated on my shoes to stop the spinning, and reached for his forearms. I leaned back into him and stepped back off the wall, so grateful not to be in danger anymore, as if someone other than I myself had put me there.

Willis would have joined me rather than stopped me. Laszlo would have started shouting. Neither John nor Alec would have left the party.

So that's where I was when Ted called to ask me to stay. Safe in his arms.

After the robbery I wanted him in my bed, pinning me down in his heavy way. I wanted it more powerfully than I had in years. That's what making love with Ted did. It nailed me in place. He penetrated me like a pin through a butterfly. There *you are*, said his thrust. *I know exactly who you are, and you're right* there.

On

Getting out

of Bed

I hope Zoë can have that feeling with a man one day. Poor young thing. She called me recently from Milan, lost and crying. She took a job there when her relationship with her boyfriend fell apart, and she's finding it very difficult on her own. "You have to build up a pile of rocks," I told her. "These hard times are when you build the pile of rocks in your soul," I said. And then the air in my body stopped moving. It always does that when I calculate the age my child would be if I'd had it. Twenty-seven. A couple of years had gone by since the last time I'd counted, since I'd admitted that I could be a grandmother. I can't help doing the calculation when Zoë is sad, or when she asks me rather than Judy for advice. My breath stops, and I see a girl, I see a boy, I see a mirage that shimmers first as a young woman, then as a young man. I closed my eyes and breathed hard and jump-started my lungs. "Make them immovable," I said with some force. "Then you can lean on them later."

She seemed to understand. It's a wonder she hasn't consoled herself with a romantic Milanese yet. I didn't recommend it, but I think I will next time we talk. She says it's really hard to concentrate at work. I know. I know.

Sometimes, when I don't have to be at the office, I can't get out of bed. I have plenty of rocks in my soul, but they are there for emotional reassurance. They can't do my taxes for me, or decide on birthday presents. It's odd: When there's a man in my bed, I get up. I pee and wash, and make coffee. I look through the fruit bowl for pieces that aren't starting to rot. I bring in the paper, or even go out and get one if I know which one he prefers. Alone, though, there are days I do none of these things, except maybe pee. Coffee can wait. I just can't get up. How strange that you can love being in bed so much and hate yourself so much at the same time. I had one of these mornings a few weekends ago. I let my mind wander for hours. The cat was also zoned out, undemanding. I studied the set of drawers in the corner for a while. I started thinking I should have painted them. White. The thick particleboard had seemed a pleasant tan color, sort of Scandinavian, and I'd been in too much of a hurry to put all my panties and stockings in the drawers to wait for paint to dry. I'll do it someday. When I retire, probably, because I'll end up looking at it more often then.

Lying in bed that awful, dark day, I thought about Mother as I had last seen her: lying in bed, in the hospital.

I never knew her to sleep in; the day simply had to begin. If she stayed upstairs longer than Poppa, it was because she never came downstairs without her hair set and her powder and lipstick on. Corky's mother didn't do this, and Corky said to me once when she slept over during high school that it was amazing that Mother did, given that she'd grown up on a farm, and I said, no, it was *because* she'd grown up on a farm. Of that much I was sure. In her hospital bed, though, she had just a little worn-out makeup on. She had fallen down the stairs; a broken rib had punctured a lung. George Junior and Judy had just dropped Zoë off at college in Chicago and had driven on down to Columbia for a visit. They'd turned into the driveway behind an ambulance. I was pulled out of a meeting to take the call. George Junior said, "I think you better hurry, Lil," so I did.

When I arrived in the hospital room and went straight to Mother to tell her I was there, I wanted to put fresh lipstick on her. I was so sure it would make her feel better. It would make all of us feel better. There wasn't time, though. "Mother," I said, holding her brittle arm through the sheet, "it'll be all right." She turned her strained and weary eyes toward me. George Junior came up behind me and told me Mother couldn't talk. She blinked very slowly, and a large tear rolled down her cheek. Why? Because there was to be no more lipstick? But there was. I chose the shade for the undertaker.

Lipstick is very important, but it doesn't get me out of bed any more than coffee does. After thinking about Mother's death in bed that dark day, I came back to myself and stared at the pile of clothes on the chair in the corner. I'd spent so much time agonizing over the fabric and so much money having the chair reupholstered and now it was covered in blouses and there was nothing I could do about it. I couldn't even turn on my side and look at something else. I couldn't find the energy anywhere in my body. But eventually I got hungry. After tolerating the hunger for a while my mind walked into the kitchen and looked into the fridge and remembered I was out of eggs, and eggs were all I wanted. So I got up. Around three, I think. I got the idea to go uptown to the supermarket. I could have walked over to the 7-Eleven for half a dozen, but I wanted a dozen. And they say the supermarket isn't a bad place for singles to meet. The *Times* even did a short feature on it. The best place is the frozen food section, I understand. It's probably mostly true for the younger singles, but you never know. Why wouldn't an elegant older fellow, perhaps a widower, take himself to the supermarket at the beginning of the weekend? He might have a housekeeper during the week, but might enjoy the walk to the store from time to time, to buy a paper and a pastry, maybe, or a bottle of wine.

I'm trying to remember if Pyam ever did his own shopping. I don't think he did. I'm so glad that dwindled to nothing, that connection. He was such a stringy man. And not fully a widower either. His wife was bedridden after a terrible stroke, and had been for years. So I was his companion; I was on his arm. He didn't cut a bad figure at all, but eventually I wondered how much of this perception really had to do with his late father's legacy rather than Pyam's own character and posture. When the father changes the face of American diplomacy, it turns out to be impossible to think of the son as anything but a son. Never fully grown.

When I look back now on that relationship, I remember how I thought I benefited. I mean, we went out so often, there was clearly something that kept me saying yes. I think I was trying to convince myself that pleasant conversation in sophisticated company was enough. Ted was gone and I couldn't expect anything like him again. That's what I must have been telling myself. I remember that I enjoyed dressing for diplomatic dinners. But under my dress I was still in withdrawal, gasping for a fix of passion.

Once, when Pyam invited me to his home for a simple dinner after a consular cocktail reception, he told me he'd like to take me up to meet his wife. I'd met Ted's wife many times. How not to, as his PA? How not to talk to her on the phone on a weekly basis? This was different, though. This meeting felt more professional than meeting Ted's wife ever had.

We didn't climb a narrow gothic staircase to an attic room, but we did have to go up to the third floor of the slender house, where two rooms and a toilet had been fitted out for his wife and her live-in nurse. As I went up the stairs I realized I was a sort of assistant to Pyam, keeping society from pitying his situation. I wonder if he imagined he was doing the same for me.

Her room was very pretty. Chintz, and a clean, pale carpet. The bedside light was unfortunately frilly, but it threw a warm light. Pyam sat on a chair by the bed and I stood. "Claire, this is Lillian," he said to her collapsed face. Her one bright eye turned to me, and I said, "Hello, Claire. I'm very happy to meet you." She looked at me a bit longer, then what she wanted to say seemed to take form deep down in her body, and it set her shaking as it moved up into her throat and then her mouth. She thrust the working part of her mouth forward. "Lovely," she said, then she looked back at Pyam.

"We've been to the British consulate this evening,

Claire," he said. He wasn't holding her hand, just leaning toward her with his elbows on his knees. He gave her a brief account of the evening, naming the people there she knew, then he told her we'd be having some supper in the kitchen. He stood up and looked at me, so I told her good night. He went ahead of me down the stairs. I looked at the wrinkled depression at the base of his skull, above his fine suit and the spotless collar of his dress shirt. That evening was definitive for me. He was an upstanding man, but he was through and through as dry as the kisses I received on the cheek after each outing. Claire had had his youth. I didn't want his old age.

Going home that evening, I wondered if I would look for a platonic escort of my age if I were in Pyam's position. I decided not. I'll always want someone whose fingers are strong enough to pull my hair. Always. So I now have Michael. And anyway, escorting is what gay friends are for.

I didn't just get out of bed on that dark day a few weeks ago. I got up, I got dressed, and I went to the supermarket. No luck, but I felt better for having put myself out on the firing range. And then I had eggs in the fridge, which is so much better than not having them.

On Fate

Having is better than not having. There's just not enough time sometimes. Often. People don't give it to you. They sleep too long. Or life doesn't give it. The Fates don't. I'm completely with the Greeks on that. The Fates spin your life's thread, tie it up in knots for fun, and when they think it's the right length, they snip it, moving on. When people talk about changing their fate, I always want to laugh. If you're going to talk at all about being fated, then that's that. If you "change" your fate, then you were fated to change your fate. The words cancel each other out.

The one thing I didn't want the Fates to fool around with was my relationship with Poppa. It was so good. I never understood why he didn't want to come and live with me after Mother died. I visited him five times, and I asked him every time.

The first time, we were about to have breakfast. Poppa was sitting at the dining table with the paper, and I was in the kitchen. It was summer, and the sun was shining in through the windows, but even so, the kitchen didn't feel alive. I opened the old fridge, feeling it rock in a way I didn't remember, and found English muffins, butter, and the apricot jam I'd sent down in a care package. There was an unopened deli packet of ham on a shelf, dated ten days before, and there were a few rubbery potatoes in the salad drawer. I put the muffins in the toaster and took the top off the milky white Pyrex butter dish. The butter inside was bright yellow, and crumbled like soft chalk when I pressed the knife into it. It was the right color in the middle, and it took a long greasy time to cut the outside away and spread only the good stuff on the muffins. I doubted Poppa would even notice the difference in the butter himself. He'd spread it no matter what color it was, and he'd cover it with jam, and he'd eat it. Maybe he'd get sick. Then what would he do?

I opened the jam and put it on a saucer with a spoon so he could serve himself, and took that and the plate of muffins out to the dining room. The dining room didn't look dead. Dining tables and sideboards never look like their time has come and gone like fridges do, not as long as they've got all four legs. Poppa folded up the paper to make space for the food, and patted my hand when I sat down.

"Anything interesting?" I said.

"Nothing I'll remember for long," he answered, and pulled the jam toward him. I watched him put a big dollop on his first muffin half. Seeing him anticipate the first mouthful gave me the same feeling I had when I had fed John's children. They'd always wanted me to eat too, so I'd pretended to, but mostly I'd just watched them chew and swallow and study what to attack next.

"I'd like to be able to sit and watch you put jam on your muffin every morning, Poppa," I said. He chuckled a little, and leaned over his plate to eat. Old age had collapsed his handsome straight nose and made it whistle, and he nearly got the tip of it daubed with apricot. I needed to come at the subject another way. My mouth was dry. "If you came to live with me," I said while he chewed, "I'm sure we could get the *Post-Dispatch* delivered to my apartment for you."

He swallowed, and then he looked me in the eye for the first time that morning. "Don't give up on me yet," he said.

"Give up on you? Poppa! How can you think that's what I'm doing? I'm not giving up on you! I'm celebrating you!" God, that was so upsetting, that first conversation! "I'm rejoicing in you, Poppa," I said as he took another bite of his breakfast and patted me on the hand again, looking straight ahead, chewing. "You wouldn't be putting me out, you know," I said, in case that was his concern. "Not at all. It would be no burden at all to have you with me." He just smiled.

"I like it here, Lillian," he said.

For a moment I had an image of throwing out all my furniture and moving all Mother and Poppa's up to New York, so he could still wake up and sit at that table, and make drinks in the evening at that sideboard. Then he said it was time to go to church.

He had always been the one to drive, so he drove us there, and only gently bumped the car behind us when he parked. At church he exchanged warm greetings with people who'd known him for decades, which was a bit of a consolation, so I didn't bring the subject up again until the cancer had been confirmed and I flew down again.

Which was harder, asking him the first time, or asking him the last time? That initial rejection wasn't easy: that "I like it here" that meant nowhere else would do, not even the home I would make for the two of us. But the last time, the visit before I went down for his colon surgery . . . No one should have to experience a conversation like that. We were at the dining table again. I'd made sandwiches he'd hardly touched. We'd been having a sweet conversation about Mother. I'd asked him to remind me where they met, and he'd said, "At church, I guess," and then went on to describe how he would visit with her on the porch of her parents' home. He told me how the wicker love seat creaked, so they tried to sit stock-still even when he kissed her. We laughed at that, and then I blurted out, "Maybe I could get us a place with a porch, outside the city, and a couple of rocking chairs," and that shut him down. He pushed back his chair, and then he put his knuckles on the table to heave himself up to stand, and the effort made him let loose into his adult diaper with a sound so embarrassing for him my heart broke in two. He made his way to the stairs, and I sat in the dining room with the smell he left behind hanging around me like a reprimand. I listened to him climb the stairs and close the door to his bathroom. I sat and cried, knowing that he was changing his own soiled diaper in the bathroom he'd been using all his married life, the bathroom he'd read the daily news in, and watched television in, and shaved himself clean and handsome in.

Later I'd go up and light a match, and flap and refold his towels, like Mary had taught me.

I don't know how I managed it, for those two years between their deaths, knowing that he was alone in Columbia, diapered, running the Cadillac through red lights, sorting through a dozen types of medication with his clumsy hands. It was a nightmare. There were times I wished he'd have a minor traffic accident to force the discussion again, but I scared myself doing that because he might hurt someone else in the process. I don't think you can actually desire things in a specific degree. You can wish for an accident or no accident. You can't wish for a minor loss of control, some damaged garbage cans and a dented fender. If he'd had a little accident like that, though, George Junior certainly would have been able to get him to be reasonable and give up the house and move in with me. Did he think it would be disloyal to Mother? I would have made him see that it wasn't just an ending but also a beginning. And also a middle, actually. A more involved relationship with me—where's the ending in that?

Beginnings are crystal clear. Endings are too, once they're final. It's always difficult to tell what part of the middle you're in, though. This morning I decided that if Michael walked into the kitchen and said he thought it best that we stop meeting like this, then it would be the beginning of the end. If he didn't, that would mean we're still at some unspecified part of the middle. He didn't. It's wonderful that he's started coming back to New York regularly. There's never been any mention of a plan to end his marriage. We don't pretend to be in love. All the same, I think I'd like him here more often. I don't mention it, though, since that might be the end, or the beginning of the end.

Relationships don't end when you stop seeing each other

and talking to each other. I think you have a relationship—
you as an individual have a relationship with someone—as
long as the memory of him plucks a string on your heart. In
the beginning of the end, that string is still very taut. Your
body resonates and people can see the effect of hearing his
name vibrate through you. Over time, the string gets looser,
and plucking it has a weaker response. You avoid plucking,
because the sound it makes is less and less beautiful as it
goes slack. The relationship is over when thoughts of him
don't send your fingers out to the guitar at all.

On Overflowing

What month is it now? April? Oh God, I have to do my taxes. *God.* I was going to clear up my desk before now, so I'd be ready. Something happened. There was the board meeting. I had a brunch for my London and Paris colleagues. I stayed up late boiling and peeling and deviling dozens of eggs. Yes. It was such a great party. I can't believe I ever left Europe. I thought I'd make some more deviled eggs this morning, so that if Michael walked in he'd see I wasn't just waiting for him. But something happened. I did something else. Can't remember what now.

April. The pool will open in about ten weeks. That's good. That's really good. Feels like forever, but it's some consolation. I swim my laps, and I sit in the sun, right in the sun, and I watch all the bizarre people come and go, different every time I'm there. Maybe there will be some more regulars like me this year, maybe a bachelor or two. I always wonder what it would take for that to happen. It seems to me the chances of a middle-aged bachelor joining the pool for the summer should be pretty high, but it hasn't occurred. What would it take to improve those chances? What part of the cosmos needs a nudge? In the meantime I watch the people, and wonder why they feel comfortable in the bathing suits they've chosen. You won't see me there in twenty years with my skin flowing like lava out of my suit. And you won't see me there this year in a bikini. So many women don't realize that a bikini often makes their bodies less attractive than their naked selves. The skin bunches and folds. I guess some women actually know this but don't care. Which is worse, not realizing or not caring? I haven't decided. I don't know. Extra skin is awful.

Extra feeling is awful too. It hangs out beyond the edges of the relationship. Edges are so sad. It seems that the edges should be the problem, but then I always end up feeling that the feelings are. But they're not like lasagna noodles. You can't just cut them off when they don't fit in the pan you've chosen. I'm doing pretty well with Michael, keeping everything in the pan. It's a small pan, with feelings to match. And the sex is fine. Not stunning. Fine. So it fits in the pan too.

At least there's a pan. At least there's sex in it.

I need it so much. Do most people pretend not to? I can't lie down at night without feeling my body drag at me for it, like a child pulls on its mother's arm when they pass a toy store. Strange that it's okay if I lie on my side, but on my back it's unavoidable. My breasts whisper against my nightie, my pubis wakes up, egged on by the bone it's supposed to sleep on. This isn't supposed to be happening at my age. I can't get any reading done, and when I give in, I cry afterward. And now I want to have it again. I don't know when Michael has to end this visit. I forget what he told me, if he told me. Every morning I let him sleep, and I know I *should* let him sleep, but I always wonder how he'd feel about me waking him up with a hot kiss. I hate that I can't be sure. I hate the constant wondering. I feel like I'm dissolving. Or dispersing. I'm a dandelion and my fluff is gone, carried away on the slipstream of the people who've left. And now I'm just a stalk, pretending I've still got fluff, pretending that I'll plant my seeds where I choose to when I choose to, but in reality it's too late, they've already blown away, and they landed on Ted, and they haven't come back.

On the
End

I absolutely want more of this and less of that," Ted said. He said it three times in about twelve hours. The first time, we were in a cab on our way out to dinner. I was tired, and was leaning my forehead against his so familiar but always shocking shoulder. "That" was Florence. His wife. The second time he said it we were in my bed. The third time was the following morning. I was in my nightie making coffee; he was in a bathrobe that he kept in my closet. Each time he said it he said it the same way, emphasizing the word *absolutely*. The first two times I didn't say anything. The third time, though, I turned and looked at the big man I'd loved for nearly twelve years, and he was looking right back at me. "Absolutely?" He nodded. We'd been through this before, and of course the first handful of times I had thrown myself into his arms, and then we got bogged down in the details and weeks, months, years passed. This time I stayed where I was. The coffee started dripping. "How?"

I couldn't believe what I heard him saying. This time there wasn't just feeling; this time there was a plan. He'd taken early retirement over a year before, you see, at sixty-three. They were still living in New York, but the paper-work was nearly all done for the apartment he'd bought for Florence in Vail, like she'd always wanted. She imagined they'd both be going, of course, but he'd tell her the truth, make her agree to go on her own. He'd stay in New York with me and the hell with the rest. "The hell with 'em," he said. "Give me some coffee."

Then he went home and had a stroke.

I learned secondhand, of course, nearly a week after the fact. Someone in the mailroom had finally thought to ask whether he might actually want the copies of *Foreign Affairs* that continued to arrive for him. They asked Olivia from reception to call. What if they'd asked me? Would I have been able to call? He left my apartment to go home and reveal his plans to Florence. That's what I thought he had done. That's why I believed I hadn't heard from him. I couldn't have called his home in the middle of that effort. Things were complicated. He needed time to make it work.

Imagining that lasted a day or two. For several silent days after that I fought against the possibility—hulking silently like a boulder in the field I was cultivating, ready to ruin my plowshare—that once again he wasn't going to fol-low through. And then I passed reception on my way to the toilet and Olivia said to me, "Lillian, have you heard about Mr. Bishop? Poor thing's in the hospital. Talked to his wife this morning." And she rattled on, and I walked backward while I listened, hoping it looked like I was concerned but also that I really had to pee, and then I excused myself and turned and fled to the ladies'.

Three more weeks passed. Someone told me he'd gone home from the hospital. A couple of people asked me if I knew anything, imagining that I'd have called to talk to get details from Florence, and I just said, "Nothing new to report, I'm afraid." I chewed the top layer of skin off my lips. I ripped my cuticles to shreds.

Oh, the excitement and the despair when he finally called! I had to calm down. I had so many questions, but he had trouble talking. I had to simplify.

"Can you say 'yes,' Ted?" I asked.

"Ya," he said.

"And 'no'?"

Pause. "Na."

So, closed questions would lead him to my door.

"Are you at home?"

"Ya."

"Can I meet you somewhere?"

Pause. "Na."

"Can you come over sometime?"

Pause. "Ya."

"This evening?"

Pause. "Na."

"Sunday?"

Pause. "Na."

"Monday?"

"Ya."

"Evening?"

"Na."

"Lunch?"

"Ya."

I forgot and asked him how he'd come over, and his answer was a three-second nightmare, a record played backward, a raving, slobbering lunatic, and I interrupted, "Shall I send a cab for you?"

Pause.

"Ya. Ya."

I could feel his relief that I'd come up with a plan. I could feel it. I knew him that well.

I took Monday off. Ted came to the door with a walker and when I opened the door he tried to pull his face upward into a smile, and he tried to say my name—I know that's what he was trying to do, but it came out like a bark, just like it had on the phone. Bark, bark . . . bark. But it was Ted. It wasn't winter but he came in a coat, and I took it off his bent body, undoing the buttons with a tenderness he would never have given me time for in the past. I guided him to his chair. Not where other men sit. I always put Ted at the head of the table. We sat down to boiled new potatoes, a fillet of sole, and a salad of endives. There was butter and lemon by our plates, and I started to cry. All the questions I wanted to ask, all the massive, massive backlog of desire and frustration welled up in my throat, hot as magma, then overflowed. He thumped my forearm with his big hand. I put my head on that hand and sobbed. I waited for the other hand to reach over and stroke my head like Poppa would have done, but Ted couldn't manage it. The trip from the elevator to my door must have been an eternity. I looked up. "I wish you'd had them call me from downstairs," I blurted. "I could have walked along the hall with you." Ted snorted, like a bull. And he was right. You leave a man alone to do what he can. But he couldn't cut his food, so I did. He had a system after that: He laid his left index finger along the edge of his plate, and pushed the mouthfuls I had cut up for him against it with the fork.

I tried not to ask a lot of questions while we ate, because when he said "Ya" or "Na" the food fell about in his mouth, and out. When I could talk more calmly, I talked about the office. There was always gossip. I told him we had a journalist missing in Lithuania and he started barking again, and I'll regret bringing that up for as long as I live. After a while he pushed his plate away and left his hands on the table, so I pushed my plate aside too and took his hands in mine. The bones were still big; the muscles weren't wasted, but they had lost their electricity.

"So," I said, and couldn't make more words come out. He waited. There was no "Spit it out, Lil," no "Have we got all day?" None of it. "So is this the end?" I finally said. His bottom lip curled like a baby's does before it cries. "Na," he said definitively. I felt the same surge I had at our first embrace, his first phone call to my apartment, the first time he opened his hotel room door to me.

"You'll get better?"

Pause.

"Ya."

Then the second stroke.

Florence nursed him, when it should have been me. I waited for the secondhand news of his progress, but he didn't progress, where he was never supposed to live. He wasn't supposed to need her anymore. Seventeen months later I received the secondhand news of his death.

I blacked out. When I came to, the feeling of having nothing at all was so strong I thought I was twenty-three in Munich, new to everything, scared. I didn't recognize my bedroom. Whose newspapers were those piled on that upholstered chair? Those catalogs on the floor? Whose taste was that? I struggled forward through time, toward myself and the bed and why I was on it. My heart cramped and I nearly blacked out again. You'd think I would have remembered Ted's face and his growl and the way he flicked his wrist to check his watch, but it's so embarrassing, all I could see was paper. Paper was flying, whirling all over my mind. Letters for him to sign, minutes, memos, interview transcripts, invoices, more minutes, credit card slips, and the fluttering pages of hotel guest books. I couldn't stand it. At least this feeling got me up off the bed. I found my way to the kitchen. I knew that I had to make coffee. Coffee is an excellent stand-in for blood. I stared into the first mug until it was cold. The second one I drank, bitter, without sweetener. Then I just sat.

I had to work. During the rest of that week, papers continued to whirl. I couldn't nail them down. I was sure my colleagues were from another planet. The smallest tasks took ages. Then suddenly I found myself in my bedroom looking for a cigarette.

George Junior and Judy and Zoë had come over to see me. I couldn't keep them away any longer. I had stopped smoking cold turkey when Ted told me I tasted like the air in the subway. But now my little family was sitting in my apartment, concerned for me, with just a tinge of *Now maybe she can sort herself out and get married* emanating from George Junior and just a tinge of *Poor Lillian, but thank God this is over, I never liked him* coming out of Judy. Zoë's eyes were like saucers, taking in her older-and-hardly-wisers. I knew I had some cigarettes. Someone had left them behind. The more I looked, the harder my heart beat. I couldn't go back out to the living room without one. I found them behind the iron and pulled one out. I crossed through the living room to light it with the kitchen matches, the family watching as I went. Then I pulled a chair from the dining table over to where they were sitting—far enough away to keep the smoke out of their faces—sat down, crossed my legs, felt the impassivity of my face, concentrated on the cigarette, listening to the tiny crackle of burning paper as I inhaled, blowing away from their willing-to-do-what-was-needed faces, keeping ash off the skirt of my dress.

I don't remember what was said. Judy told me later that she had brought Zoë along to show her what grief looked like. Does it look like what it feels like? Grief on the outside:

tall, middle-aged woman, dramatic eyebrows, excellent wool dress, excessively composed, unable to form sentences of more than three words. Grief on the inside: tall, middle-aged woman, imagining shaving her head, taking off the dress and the stockings, removing her breasts and folding them away in the underwear drawer with her bra, untangling her pubic hair and pulling it all out, dropping it from her bedroom window down nine floors into the dead space behind, drinking only water, never talking again, smoking until it's all over.

On What
Happens
Next

I don't think you have to know what happens next. I imagine all sorts of futures, but I've learned to swim with the tide, and to get out of the water when it's really too dangerous, or flat and uninspiring. I stand on the shore, aching to feel it on my skin again, watching for changes in the surf. I keep champagne in the hall closet to celebrate when it's time to dive back in.

There was a weekend, it must be eight years or so ago now, when one of my old beaux from London came through town—someone I had some fun with between John and Alec. Nothing serious. It was terrific to see him so many years later. He'd kept himself fit, I could feel it when we hugged at my door, could see it when he took off his sweater after our brunch of eggs Benedict. We followed the sun into the study, bringing the last of the champagne with us. When we both wanted more I said I had at least half a dozen in the closet. Neither of us cared that they wouldn't be chilled. I went to get one and put another in the fridge. I remember the giddy walk from the closet to the kitchen, and how I laughed when I went back into the study. He'd taken the cushions off the sofa and had put them on the floor in the squares of sun thrown by the windows, and he was sitting on one, leaning back on the sofa in his shirt and socks. I laughed and handed him the dusty bottle. While he untwisted the cage, I straddled his lap. We kissed as he turned the cork, little bit by little bit. "I remember you," I said against his lips. "Oh yeah?" he said, and I felt his smile expose his teeth. "You and your anticipation games," I said. I felt his arms tighten as he gave the cork its final twist. I was ready for anything. Anything, except for that listless little *pop*.

"Oh," he said, and lifted the bottle to our noses. It smelled musty and bitter. "Gimme that," I said, and got up to get the one in the fridge. That one was dead too. "I have more," I said, but he said never mind, and we spent the rest of the day on the floor. At one point he was up on one elbow and he said, "There is a rule with champagne, you know. You have to drink it. You drink it, and you replenish it. Drink, replenish, drink, replenish. It's like love, Lillian."

Fifteen years before I would have basked in his words, in the way he was stroking my hair, but suddenly I'd had enough of him. It seemed to me that he was making a veiled statement about Ted and me. I wanted to shout at him, *You didn't know us! No one did! It was fresh. It was* always *fresh!* But I was too polite to put up a fight. When you protest too much they give you a look that's even more condescending than their platitudes.

When Michael goes, whether he goes for good or not, I think I know another fellow who might visit. His name is Stanley. Terrible name, and he wears bow ties too, so I was ready not to enjoy his company, but he surprised me.

Judy had come to New York to attend a fund-raising dinner for the Friends of the Metropolitan Museum of Art, and invited me along as her date. We found ourselves standing with drinks and cocktail napkins in front of a tall, deep-voiced man who said he loved art but not as much as books. He had a charming twinkle in his eye I felt like investigating, and he smelled good. I couldn't place the cologne, and I usually can. He inclined himself toward me, and toward Judy too, I suppose, as she was standing next to me, and said, "What is it you find yourself reading the most?" It was such a surprise question, which is my favorite kind, and I'm usually very good at answering, especially at dinner parties, but it took me a while this time, because I love so many types of books, all types of books, that I didn't know where to start, and then Judy jumped in.

"Lillian reads periodicals. She keeps very up to date."

I could have wrung her neck. Even though the gentleman went on to ask me which newspapers I took and which magazines I favored, and on the surface we had a very pleasant conversation, I was so angry I found a way to get her alone when we were called to dinner.

"Why did you say that about the periodicals?" I asked her.

"Well, you do read them. You read them the most," she said.

"I read lots of things," I said. "In college they would always find me sleeping in the stacks because I couldn't stop reading."

"That was forty years ago, Lillian. You get two fat papers every day now and you let them pile up in anticipation of a day when you'll actually get through more than a half a dozen pages."

"Whenever it was, it was still me. I'm still that girl in the stacks, Judy," I said, but I was speaking to her back. She went around to the other side of the table and sat down, opening up her napkin very primly, smiling at the men on either side of her and investigating the soufflé on her plate. The gentleman in the bow tie—Stanley—pulled out my seat so I could sit, which was some sort of consolation. No one had pulled out Judy's chair.

Here's what I want you to learn from this: Never let someone answer a question for you. Jump in with anything at all to make sure that you're the one talking. Say, "That's an interesting question," or "I'm glad you asked that question," or "Oh goody! My favorite subject!" Say anything that will guarantee that you're in the conversation about yourself, and not out of it like a teenager standing next to her mother at a cocktail party.

You must tell your own story. Never let someone, even someone as familiar to you as your sister-in-law, think she knows you better than you know yourself. She only sees what you *do*; she doesn't see who you are inside. If I regret anything when I look back, it's how often I allowed people to think what they wanted to think. I should have stopped them short. I should have laughed at their assumptions. I should have hooted with laughter, "Hoo hoo hoo!" and followed with a twinkling, mischievous smile, just to throw them off, just to keep them guessing. The problem is, they watch what you do, who you love, how you cook, what you read and what you don't read, and they decide what it means, and sometimes you're not there to stop them, or you get the timing wrong. I've always wondered why people look so much to action for meaning. When people tell you a story— something that happened to them, something important— don't ask them what they did. Ask them what they *wanted* to do. What they want to do is who they are. Actions are whispers compared to dreams.

ACKNOWLEDGMENTS

Early encouragement and improvements for this book came from my gracious first-draft readers. Thank you, Charlotte Chiew, Tremaine du Preez, Alicia Erian, Hussein Khalifa, David Klopfenstein, Alyssa Landry and Nicole Stinton.

Thank you also, Andy Gurnett, for having me print and bind the manuscript so that you could read it like a book. Thank you for the interesting reflections that followed. And thank you, more than I can say, for proposing marriage.

If my mother weren't the writer Valerie Lester, I wouldn't have the sense of adventure that writing entails. If my brother weren't the writer Toby Lester, I wouldn't have such steady counsel in the wobbly times. If my agent weren't Barney Karpfinger, whose ideas keep me lively and whose wisdom keeps me calm, I'd still be writing in isolation.

Acknowledgments

Thanks also to The Karpfinger Agency's Cathy Jaque for careful scrutiny and recommendations, and to Marc Jaffee, who read it there first.

I am gleefully indebted to Amy Einhorn. Thank you for your encouragement, your galvanizing energy and your clarifying insights. Thanks also to Liz Stein for being such a cheerful guide through the process, and to everyone at Putnam for the professional excellence there.

ABOUT THE AUTHOR

Alison Jean Lester was born in the United States, and has variously grown up, studied, worked, written, and raised her two children in the United States, the United Kingdom, China, Italy, Taiwan, Japan, and Singapore. She currently lives with her family in Singapore.